HELL ON EARTH

a novel by

Shawn D. Brink

Contact: editors@gabrielshornpress.com

Published in Minneapolis, Minnesota by Gabriel's Horn Publishing

Publisher's Note: This novel is a work of fiction. Names, characters, places, and incidents are either products of the author's imagination or used fictitiously. All characters are fictional, and any similarity to people living or dead is purely coincidental.

Cover design: Gabriel's Horn Press

Cover Image: © Taily_sindariel | Dreamstime.com

First printing December 2016

Printed in the United States of America

For sales, please visit www.gabrielshornpress.com

ISBN 10: 1-938990-26-9

ISBN 13: 978-1-938990-26-7

DEDICATION

I dedicate this book to all the readers of fiction. You are the wind in my sails and without you I would be dead in the water.

ACKNOWLEDGEMENT

Before all else, I thank God, for without Him, this trilogy would be an impossibility.

A special thanks to Laura Vosika and her staff at Gabriel's Horn Press. An author could not ask for better people to work with. Without them, this book would not be what it is.

I would also like to thank Laurie Kehoe, who co-wrote the novel *A Dream of Dragons* with Michael Kehoe. Laurie referred me to Gabriel's Horn Press and without her referral, who knows what would have become of this trilogy.

Lastly, I would like to thank my wife and children for putting up with me while I wrote and wrote and wrote and wrote and wrote and wrote and wrote and… well you get the picture.

Part One

Seeker's Salvation Day

CHAPTER 1

Bob looked out over the hundreds that had gathered on the main grounds. He felt giddy as he looked them over. He had summoned them. They had come. Of course they came! He was their unquestioned leader. He was Robert Gulam, First Seeker and leader of the Union of Seekers.

The crowd quieted as he approached the podium. Recollections of old Hitler footage came to mind as he stood before his loyal masses. Of course, he wasn't Hitler, but the vibe was similar, and his followers were as loyal as any Nazi who ever lived. Plus, like Hitler, he was bent on conquest, albeit through more successful avenues.

"Greetings," he began, as a slight squeal of feedback reverberated through the PA system. He glanced at the one operating the media booth. Their eyes locked momentarily before the young man jumped into action and made the required adjustments. The feedback faded away. The young man gave him two thumbs up and Bob resumed his posture.

He looked out over the crowd. If a pin had dropped at that moment, it would have sounded like a clap of thunder.

He raised both hands in the air and gave the greeting his followers were waiting to hear. "How high do you roll?"

The roaring response hit him like a tidal wave. "As high as we can."

Bob frowned. It should have been 100% unison on the response, but it was just short of that. He quickly zeroed in on the chain's weak link—a man standing near the front of the crowd, who had failed to give the proper response. He'd tried, but his lips moved a second behind everyone else's.

Had Bob been anyone else, such a minute detail may have gone unnoticed, but he was no average man. He was an enlightened Seeker. Every Seeker knew this greeting and would recite the response on cue without hesitation. So why did this man hesitate? Bob smelled a rat. He narrowed his eyes at this outlier. He didn't recognize him—strike one.

"Today we are few," Bob continued while keeping a keen eye on the suspected impostor. "But a few is enough!"

The eruption of cheers was deafening. The alleged impostor joined in, but seemed unsure why he was cheering—strike two.

"We have more numbers to our ranks than you may know!" Again ruckus from the crowd engulfed his words. "I have been visited by the Ra."

The ruckus disappeared. Again, that hypothetical falling pin would have shaken the whole earth upon landing. *Of course they were silent,* Bob thought. *They don't understand.*

He looked at the suspected impostor and smiled. The man hung on everything Bob said. So did the rest. But unlike the others, whose sole focus was on him, this man appeared to be trying to take in everything at once. After considering, Bob decided he would ignore the imposter for now. After all, *the show must go on.*

His eyes scanned his silent audience. "And who is the Ra, you ask? I'll tell you. They are the ones we have been seeking these long years." He had to wait a moment as the crowd erupted into applause. Once the din quieted to manageable levels, he continued. "The Ra is an interdimensional race of beings who are far superior to us in virtually every way. In fact, they created us as a species many millennia ago through a genetic experiment. They are our creators, our gods, if you wish to look at them in that light."

Silence greeted his words.

It was strange to him, this contrast between the moments of rowdy cheering and intense silence. At this moment, silence reigned. Maybe it was to be expected as his followers digested this new information. It was huge news, after all, a proverbial bombshell. The whole purpose of the Union of Seekers had been to discover the truth relating to gods or goddesses in the universe. Now he was proclaiming the discovery of that truth.

He raised his voice, calling across the crowd. "One of the Ra spoke to me. His name is Splinter. He told me to gather the Union and wait here for them to return." Bob thought the previous silence was the most intense possible. Now he knew he had been wrong. Immersed in this ultra-intense quiet, he could hear his own heart beating, like a pair of crashing cymbals reaching a crescendo.

He looked over the silent crowd and said, "That is all." He backed away from the podium. He descended the steps of the stage knowing the eyes of every Seeker followed him. He didn't look at them, but he knew they were watching. He could feel the energy of their stares, their chi, their life-force.

Among the crowd, he walked directly to the suspected impostor. Face to face, he sized him up. They were about the same height and build, although the other was noticeably younger, maybe by as much as thirty years.

"So," Bob said as a smile grew on his face. "How high do you roll?"

"As high as I can?" the man answered.

Bob's smile faded. This was the correct answer. But the man had said it almost as a question, unsure of his response. That would be the case, if the man had heard the statement for the first time only moments earlier.

"Well said," Bob lied.

The man nodded.

"Sir, can you please show me your credentials?"

"Um…" was the man's reply.

Bob's smile reappeared. He was moving in on the kill. "You know, your proof of membership."

The man said nothing, but his fear-laden eyes told Bob all he needed to know.

"That's okay," Bob said. Then he raised his voice, addressing all those in hearing range. "Can anyone else here show me what I meant by 'credentials'?"

In unison, the crowd held up, as high as they could reach, their credentials. Every one of them presented their three dice.

Bob's grin was now so large it strained his facial muscles. "It appears you are without your dice. Did you happen to forget them?"

The man did not answer.

"We never forget our dice, never." Bob still smiled, but the friendliness in his voice had grown scarce.

The man took a nervous step back—a mistake, Bob thought. *You never back away from a predator.*

"Okay," the man said. "Here's the deal. I'm not a member of your group."

"Then why are you here?" Bob asked pleasantly.

"I'm a member of the free press."

"I don't follow," said Bob.

"I'm a news reporter." He hesitated, then continued. "Mr. Gulam, are you aware that many mainstream Americans consider your group to be a cult?"

"Really?" Bob feigned interest.

"And a dangerous cult at that."

Bob saw where this conversation was headed, but allowed it to continue. He wanted to hear what this newsman had to say.

"Furthermore, are you aware there's a federal investigation concerning your group?"

"An investigation?" Bob acted shocked even though he knew.

"Yes. An investigation. A known member of your group recently tried to kill an infant at a business known as Millie's House of Witchcraft."

Bob reacted calmly. "People have free will sir. They make their own choices. I certainly don't make them on their behalf."

"The gun that was used in the attempted murder was a stolen weapon and the authorities have traced it back to you."

Bob went stiff. He didn't care that the weapon had been traced even though all of the Union's stolen weapons had gone through modifications designed to minimize that risk. He did however note the man's choice of words. "Did you say attempted?" If Quincy had failed, that was a large and hairy fly in his ointment.

"I did say that. The perp was a young man attending college in Santa Fe, but who had recently been to your compound according to my sources. Luckily, he was killed before he could commit the murder."

Bob's heart sank. He didn't give a flying fart about Quincy. That useless excuse for a man was expendable. He did however worry how this affected the Ra. He wondered if Splinter had been harmed as well. He wondered how this would affect the overall plan. He hoped not. Concerned with what else this man might say, yet unable to let it go, he asked, "Is there anything else?"

Now it was the man's turn to grin. "There's more. The owner of the business was found dead in the basement. She had been disemboweled. But you're trying to get me off topic aren't you, Mr. Gulam?"

Bob shook his head.

The reporter dove into his questions. "Mr. Gulam, do *you* consider your group to be a cult?"

"Define 'cult.'"

"Certainly. A cult, by definition is…"

The gun fired. The reporter stopped yammering. The 38 caliber bullet had blown his mouth clean off his face.

Bob always carried. He doubted this reporter knew that about him, and now it was too late.

For a moment, the reporter stared blankly at Bob. He blinked once, the remains of his mouth opening and closing like a fish out of water. Then he collapsed to the ground, unmoving.

Bob stood over him, the warmth from his still-smoking gun cozying up his palm. He looked up from the one-time investigative reporter, now nothing but worm-food, to stare at his followers. Pride welled up in him. They had witnessed what was necessary. He knew none of them would question his wisdom in committing this act.

"Open his shirt," he ordered.

Buttons popped. The shirt opened. Bob saw something he hoped he would not see.

"Well, that's too bad," he exclaimed. "But then, I expected nothing less from the media."

He reached down and grabbed the wire taped to the body's shaved chest and put the small microphone to his lips.

"Listen up. Your boy here has had an unfortunate accident. He might be late to his scheduled rendezvous." He chuckled, and added, "I think he's decided to stay with us for a while." He dropped the microphone and smashed it under the heel of his boot. Then, he looked out at the crowd.

On most of their faces, he saw surprise—surprise, but not fear. That was good. Fear was debilitating and something they could not afford. He thought of the future. More killing was eminent. The war was about to begin.

CHAPTER 2

Moses was a foreigner. At least that was what everyone had always told him. His appearance confirmed it and yet, this was home and it had been ever since he could remember.

His foreign status was evident. The natives were considerably taller and much lighter in complexion. Their behavior, too, was far different than his—less expressive and more stoic.

Regardless of his foreign status, this was the only home he had ever known. He had been brought here from the far side of The Space Between while still in his mother's womb. That was almost twenty years ago.

Outer Earth was not a bad place to live. Sure, it could be gloomy. His parents said the weather was a lot like a place from their homeland, called Seattle. He had, of course never been to Seattle, as it existed on the far side of The Space Between. His parents had vacationed there once, said it was a fun place to visit, but not a place they'd want to live—too gloomy. How ironic they now lived here.

Moses looked up at the sky and at The Space Between. It existed at the separation between the normal grey sky of the land to the swamp green of the far off unknown between the Earths. He liked to gaze up at that gateway, for it was a gateway to his native land, a land he couldn't remember ever being in and yet it was his home.

"Moses." A voice interrupted his thoughts. "Your father wishes to speak with you."

Moses looked up to see Harry. "Where is he?" Moses asked. He was fluent in their language. In fact, he was more fluent in that language than in the tongue of his parents, a language they called English. Not that it mattered in Outer Earth. All languages could be understood here.

"Your father is on the far side of the camp with Carl."

Moses got up. He hoped his father would tell him it was time to head back to town. He didn't like camp. He missed civilization. Unfortunately, these days he spent way too much time in the wilds. His father always led the expeditions, searching and mapping previously unexplored wilds of Outer Earth. And their mission was always the same: search and destroy.

They were always searching for the elusive egg of the hundred-year-old beast. If it could be found and destroyed before it hatched, then perhaps the cycle could be broken and the earths could be freed from the curse that had wreaked havoc upon them for so long.

Hunter always led these expeditions, for out of all the inhabitants of the land, he was the most capable of destroying the egg. After all, he possessed *the power of five*.

Moses found his father's tent and entered. The interior consisted of one large space in the center of which stood a table holding a map. Facing each other across the table stood his father, and his father's best friend Carl.

Moses stifled a grin. His dad looked like a child next to the other.

Like Moses, Hunter was average height—for somebody from Inner Earth. This was not Inner Earth, however and the natives were what his father called professional basketball players. The comedy of the scene was accentuated by the fact that the table was too tall for his dad. The top came just below his eye-level so he could observe the map, but just barely.

Moses and his parents had become used to everything being the wrong size. It was just the way things were in Outer Earth. The natives always made an effort to make things tolerable for them, the only vertically challenged members of the tribe. For example Hunter had been provided with a step stool that he often stood upon so as to better view the map. At the moment however, he was not using it and he seemed too excited to care.

"The scout says it's been spotted here?" Hunter touched the map with his index finger.

"Ah," came Carl's response. "That is correct."

Moses cleared his throat to announce his presence and both of them looked up. As usual, he couldn't read Carl's expression. His dad's face, however, said enough for them both.

He virtually flew to his son, tripping over the unused step stool. Moses caught him in his arms. "We've found the egg!" Hunter exclaimed as he was put back on his feet by his son.

"What?" Moses could barely believe his ears.

CHAPTER 3

Word of the reporter's murder quickly became front page news. It was no surprise to Bob Gulam. It's never a good thing, after all, to kill someone who's wearing a wire. Bob shook his head as he palmed three dice in his left hand, squeezing them tightly as if by doing so, he could push back time and reverse the heinous act he had committed. Of course no such action could bring the reporter back to life and deep down, Bob was at peace with it. It was something that had to be done, an inevitable necessity.

Still, he worried what the death of the reporter meant for him and his followers. The media had caught the scent of blood. Soon they would descend like sharks, and riding on those sharks' backs would be the Feds. It was a matter of time before the situation devolved into another Branch Davidian Waco, Texas scenario. *Well, if it is a war that they want, then it is a war they will get,* he thought to himself.

He didn't fear death. It was more the inevitability of losing this war frustrated him. The Union going against the Feds was like a mosquito attacking a gorilla. You might hold your own for a bit, you might even draw some blood; but in the end the mosquito is doomed to die under the swat of the gorilla's massive hand. His frown deepened. He didn't want to go the way of David Koresh. He didn't want to be the mosquito.

His only hope was in the message from Splinter of the Ra. *Assemble the Union and wait,* Splinter had said. Of course Splinter *hadn't* told him to murder a member of the Press while waiting. That had been a spontaneous act.

Bob wondered if the Ra would approve of such a move. He had the feeling they had no problem with the Union of Seekers doing whatever was necessary to purify the human race by eliminating any doubting Thomases —which certainly included members of the Free Press. But then again, the Union didn't need this kind of heat. It was too much, too soon.

"Sir?"

Bob turned towards the one who had entered his room. "Speak."

"The Feds have surrounded the compound and they've brought the whole media-circus in tow."

It had happened faster than expected. Still, Bob was not surprised.

He dismissed the messenger and as soon as the door closed, he released the dice which he had been incessantly palming. They clattered about, bouncing and jiving as if alive.

"How high do you roll?" Bob asked himself as the dice came to a rest.

They settled. He looked. He smiled.

All three showed sixes. Everything was going to be okay.

CHAPTER 4

The expedition broke camp and set out into the wilderness. Moses walked in formation, his father on one side and Carl on the other. The rest filed in behind them.

His heart pounded. This didn't surprise him. He had a lot to be anxious about. If the scout's report could be believed, the egg of the hundred-year-old beast had been found. It was unprecedented. The location of the egg had never before been discovered. Now they knew where it was, it must be destroyed. The cycle had to be broken.

Moses looked at his dad. Then he looked at Carl. They were both stone-faced. For Carl, this was normal, but it worried him to see it in his dad. It was not his norm.

Almost as disconcerting as the lack of expression, was the lack of conversation. The whole troop marched without noise as if sound itself had fled in fear. In reality the silence was not absolute. A single noise could be heard. It just took a moment for his ears to pick it up.

"One. Two. Three. Four. Five. One. Two. Three. Four. Five. One. Two. Three. Four. Five."

Moses heard Hunter counting off steps under his breath. His dad always did things in sets of five. This compulsion held especially true when Hunter felt nervous.

His dad called it OCD—Obsessive Compulsive Disorder. According to his dad, OCD had been a curse of his back in his native land. It slowed him down and held him hostage to himself, whatever that meant.

Here in Outer Earth however, Hunter's curse had become a blessing. Here in this world, whenever he felt stressed and counted to five, his strength would multiply by that number. This made his dad a virtual super hero, able to jump five times as high, run five times as fast, and attack with five times the fury. It was quite a gift.

Moses was not fortunate enough to have inherited this blessing. It wasn't that he didn't possess OCD tendencies. He did. Apparently it was hereditary. But he'd only gotten the curse, not the blessing from it.

He listened to his father count. It drove him crazy. Five was not Moses' count of choice. For him it was three. Also, unlike his father, it was not so much a physical counting for him, but a tick in his mind. He had to blink his eyes in sets of three every time he took in new information or felt nervous. Now, he blinked and counted in his head, ticking off his sets of threes as he took in the new scenes of the unexplored lands before him.

One–two–three. One–two–three. One–two–three.

CHAPTER 5

It had been three days since the Feds had descended on the Union's compound. It was a siege Bob Gulam both invited and distained simultaneously.

Supply-wise, they were in good shape, ready for the long haul. Food, guns, ammo; they had it all in abundance. The Union members waited within their reinforced bunker walls, as prepared as they could be. There was nothing left to do but react to any move the enemy dealt out. Sooner or later, the siege would morph into a full-grown assault. It was inevitable.

Step one had begun, with the Feds trying to establish a line of communication. They had been trying for three days and, much to Bob's amusement, failing. Bob made sure their attempts were met with silence. He had no desire to communicate with his enemy. He only wanted to move to the next step. He wanted the war to begin. If he remained uncommunicative, the Feds would stop trying to talk and start trying to act. At least this was Bob's hope.

Historically speaking, the Union of Seekers' bunker was doomed to be another Jonestown or Branch Davidian compound and he was destined to be another Jim Jones or David Karesh. Still, he smiled. He had something his predecessors had not. He had the Ra on his side. The Ra had chosen the Union as their people and they would not abandon them. The triple sixes of his dice had spoken. 666 was man's number. It was his number.

In addition to the attempts to communicate, the Feds had been using another tactic. For three days, they'd been blasting music through a loud PA system. The constant bombardment of hard rock had made it difficult for the seekers to concentrate or get sleep, which had been the Fed's goal. Now, after three days, the music changed.

The high distortion guitars and insane drum beats of heavy metal was replaced by the mellow voice of John Denver as he sang with the Muppets on his famous Christmas Special. The change in tactic made Bob's smile widen. Things were progressing. The next step would soon begin.

Christmas is coming, the goose is getting fat. Time to put a penny in the old man's hat, blared Miss Piggy. Personally, he liked metal better. *Curse you John Denver. Curse you Jim Henson.* Still, his smile remained.

If you haven't got a penny, a ha' penny will do. If you haven't got a ha' penny, then God bless you. Bob picked up his uzi and slammed a full metal jacket into the grip. Things were definitely progressing.

Bob began to laugh.

CHAPTER 6

The desert sand that made up the wastes of Outer Earth stretched out before them, seemingly into infinity. Moses had noticed that the further they traveled, the quieter everything grew. Now even his father's five counts had turned internal. He could still hear him breathing in rhythm to the count, but it was no longer audible.

Moses was unsettled by the unnatural silence. It rubbed him wrong and made him wary.

According to Carl and his dad, the egg was out this direction, hidden among the expanse of untamed landscape. He thought about the significance of what they were doing and of what they were on the verge of doing. It awed him.

For time beyond memory, Outer Earthlings had searched in vain for the egg, hoping to find it and destroy it before it hatched. Never before had this quest been successful.

Now however, it seemed they were about to do what nobody had ever been able to do before. They knew the location of the egg. Now they only needed to go to it and destroy it before the beast within broke free from its shell.

But how? Could it even be done? The overwhelming consensus was that, if it could be destroyed, Hunter would be the one most likely to do so as he was the one who had previously defeated the beast itself.

A gust of wind pulled Moses from his thoughts. It seemed to come out of nowhere, carrying a plume of airborne dust up the nearest dune. He followed the mini tornado with his eyes as it rose along the slope. At the top of the dune, the dust dissipated. What was left struck him with terror. A dark figure stood there, motionless and silent. At this distance he could not make out details; only that the darkness went deeper than the black clothing the figure wore. He could feel the man watching him. Under that stare, he felt an invading blackness; black as pitch.

The wind suddenly changed directions and flung dust in Moses' face. He closed his eyes against the onslaught. When he re-opened them, the man had vanished. Moses blinked a few times, but nothing changed. The dune was vacant. He rubbed his trembling hands together, suddenly realizing how stiff and cold they had become. Gradually, the darkness within him lifted.

He began to wonder if he had actually seen what he thought he had seen. He had heard of mirages; this wilderness was known for them. Perhaps the one in black was one of those, a trick of the mind and nothing more. Something deep inside argued that what he saw was no figment of the mind. It was the watching that testified to the reality of what had been there. Those unseen but acutely felt eyes of blackness haunted him.

Should he tell his dad? He considered it, but held back, his doubt growing as the minutes ticked by. If it was nothing but a mirage, he would be a fool to tell his father.

They trudged onward, ever closer to the egg. As they passed the dune in question, Moses glanced up. He didn't want to, but terror and suspicion prompted him.

The dune remained empty.

CHAPTER 7

Bob Gulam stood in position with the loaded Uzi in his hands, pointed at the solid steel that comprised the compound's external door. Beyond the door existed a government that was no longer his. The compound rang with blasted songs of John Denver, harmonized by Kermit the Frog, and Gonzo the Great.

"Freedom of religion," he scoffed. "But no freedom for those who condemn religion."

He turned and gazed upon his army. Every Seeker from the least to the greatest stood with him, armed to the hilt and itching for a fight. He could see in their eyes their need for leadership. It was time for one of his speeches. It would be their inspiration, then he would unleash Hell.

He laid down his Uzi and picked up a megaphone so he could be heard over the incessant singing of Denver, Kermit, and Gonzo. "So," he began. "It's come down to crunch time." He had no idea what that meant exactly, but it sounded profound—the vibe he wanted. Sometimes, the vibe was more important than the actual words used.

"You are all patriots today," he called. "Patriots of a new order. I don't know how all of this is going to play out, but I know in the end, we *will* be the victors."

He grabbed his three dice from his pocket and held them high above his head. His troops did the same with theirs, a salute to the Union.

"How high do you roll?" he shouted into the megaphone.

"As high as we can!" came the monstrous reply.

Bob smiled. The energy bursting from his followers was invigorating. With their loyalties backing him, he turned back towards the door. It was go time.

CHAPTER 8

"And I saw an angel come down from heaven, having the key to the bottomless pit and a great chain in his hand. And he laid hold on the dragon, that old serpent, which is the devil, and Satan, and bound him for a thousand years." – Revelation 20:1-2.

*

Lucifer descended the dune quickly, away from the eyes of the one who had seen him—at least, he was fairly sure he'd seen him. He watched as the little band came steadily closer to the egg of the beast. He didn't fear them. Fear was something he dealt out to others. It was not something he held within. But he didn't want their attention, just yet. They were no match for him—if he was only unbound. He frowned; his power *was* bound.

His mood descended. He hated the enemy. He hated them so much. He hated their leader even more. God had always toyed with him, allowing him to use his power only in limited amounts.

He bit his lip as the rage built inside. At some point, his power would be unleashed in full force. The ancient scriptures proclaimed it and the ancient scriptures could not lie. It was his very faith in those ancient scriptures that had fooled him in the past. Time and time again, he had been led to believe his moment had come.

The first time was even before the world's creation, when he and his vast army fought against God, but it had not been his moment after all. Instead, his power was bound. He was thrown from heaven, cast out with his demonic minions, defeated in the great battle.

But a war has many battles. When God's own son died on a cross, his own father forsaking him, Lucifer felt sure he'd won. Three days later, he was proven wrong, once again played the fool for the enemy's entertainment. He'd vowed at the time, he would not be duped again. He would not be the court's jester.

His anger deepened as he remembered there *was* a third time despite his vow: his attempt to kill God's chosen, to sacrifice Alice and Kerry. Again, his power had been tethered and again he had been made the laughing stock of all creation.

His rage increased as he thought of all the other moments in between those bigger ones where he had been made the butt of cosmic jokes. He had fallen victim many times.

"Why the long face Lucifer?"

Stunned to find he was not alone, he turned to the voice. His black eyes narrowed. "Michael," he said through gritted teeth. "I was just reminiscing about the past."

Michael nodded his acknowledgment. His face remained stoic.

"Have you come to taunt me Michael?"

Michael did not answer.

"Have you come to laugh at me?"

Again, no response.

"You know how powerful I was, before the fall." Lucifer smiled. "My power was greater even than yours. Yet here and now you dare look at me face to face as if we are equals?"

"We are not equals," Michael replied, "and I dare nothing. As the Lord's General, I come on orders from on high."

Lucifer scoffed. "So you are still following around your heavenly father like some lowly pet. Tell me, are you still eating scraps from his table and lapping up water from his cupped hands?"

"I follow my King of Kings and Lord of Lords. There is none other worthy of my praise."

Lucifer sneered. "You could have joined the rebellion, Michael. At least I am my own master. I grovel to no one and I beg scraps from no one." He grinned, wider than before. "There's still time to defect. There's room in my ranks for the likes of you. I'll take you under my wing. You could be…"

"Silence!" Michael's voice boomed like thunder. "I will not sway to your temptations. They are but a chasing after the wind."

Enraged by Michael's insolence, Lucifer glared at God's general. But there was nothing he could do until his power was unbound.

"I have a message from God," Michael announced.

Lucifer became still, listening. Good or bad, a message from God deserved his attention.

CHAPTER 9

Moses marched along, focused on the dunes. The further the expedition went, the higher and more imposing they became. The dark figure had not reappeared. Moses leaned toward believing the figure had never been there at all. Yet the chill he had felt when it stood on that dune had been real enough. It had persisted; deep in his bones, a feeling those eyes still watched him from unseen shadows.

He wondered if his father and Carl felt the same. He wanted to ask, but refrained. They were close to destroying the egg of the hundred-year-old beast. If they succeeded, the searching would be over and done with. The war would be won.

If he told them now what he thought he had seen, it might put a stop to the expedition. The more he thought about it, the more he became certain that the figure was imaginary. It took considerable convincing, but he decided this would be the stand he would take. Far ahead, a gust of wind caught the desert sand. A dingy cloud formed.

He had heard of the sandstorms of this far wilderness, but he had never seen one until now. He had heard how the dust of this wasteland irritated ones skin like little burrs. They entered the storm and Moses found all the reports to be true.

The sand tortured him. They pushed onward nonetheless.

CHAPTER 10

"And cast him into the bottomless pit, and shut him up, and set a seal upon him, that he should deceive the nations no more, till the thousand years should be fulfilled: and after that he must be loosed." – Revelation 20:3

*

Lucifer stared in disbelief. He had been tricked so many times, he had grown wary of such a message. Still, it came from Michael's own lips: The time had come for the unbinding of his power!

"If this is the truth you speak as a messenger from God," he said, "then you must know what it means."

Michael nodded.

"With my powers untethered, you would do well to join me."

Michael, without hesitation, shook his head. His eyes flickered with white-hot rage.

"This will be your only chance," Lucifer said sternly. "Later, I may not be in as merciful of a mood."

"No," came Michael's single worded reply.

"Last chance?" Lucifer coaxed.

"You will never pull me to your side. My loyalties will always be with my creator."

Lucifer scoffed. "Then you are a liar. If you spoke the truth and my powers were truly being untethered, you would join me and you know it."

"You are a fool, Lucifer!" Michael's voice shook the air. "I stand here before you as a messenger of the most high God, yet you dare question me?"

Lucifer did not answer. He knew the truth. He knew God's message could be trusted. God did not lie. Still, he was confused. He could not fathom why Michael would remain loyal to his maker. Now that his powers had been freed, it was suicide not to join Lucifer's army. Lucifer stared deeply into Michael's eyes, seeking some hint of God's deception. He saw none.

"Lucifer, do you recognize these?" Michael broke the stare-down. He held out a chain and a key.

Lucifer's eyes grew wide. He did indeed recognize them: the spiritual chain that tethered his power and the spiritual key that locked him to it. It was also the key that had the power to set him free.

Michael held both items out. "The time has come, Lucifer. Take the key. Unlock your shackles. Do with them what you will."

Lucifer did not reach out and take the items. It felt too easy, as if he were a fish biting into bait. He suspected if he bit too hard, he would find the hook hidden within. He would not be trapped so easily.

"You will not take your birthright?" Michael asked.

Lucifer shook his head.

Michael sounded impatient. "God does not lie. You know this."

Lucifer was torn. He knew Michael spoke the truth. Yet, he had misgivings.

The chain and the key were thrust at him. "Take it."

Lucifer did not take it.

"Very well. If you will not take it as a gift offered, then pick it up as a dog picks up a scrap under his master's table." Michael hurled the chain and key to the ground. Upon impact, a plume of desert dust erupted, hiding the items from view.

When the dust settled, Michael had vanished. Lucifer looked down. The chain and key remained where they had landed, partially covered in the dirt. Lucifer looked up and scanned the dunes. *Where was the enemy hiding? Where had Michael gone?* As far as he could tell, he was alone. He wondered if any of this had actually occurred. He looked back down. The chain and the key remained as evidence the visitation had not been imaginary.

He picked them up—that ancient key, older than time itself. He squeezed it in his hand. It was real. He thought back to when it had been forged, back when he had first been defeated in the Great Battle, when he had been cast from his heavenly perch along with all his demon followers. That was the moment his power had first been chained.

A smile crept onto his lips. Now—finally—he had the key to unlock the chains that bound his power. He held it here in his palm, the key to his freedom. He looked down for the chain, but it was no longer in the sand. He felt pressure on his throat. The chain was on him, wrapped around his neck like a constricting serpent.

Gagging, he tried to work his fingers under the chain to release the pressure, but it was too tight. What his fingers did find, was the lock. Despite his discomfort, he was hesitant to use the key. He still suspected this was a trick being played on him for the amusement of his enemies. He wanted to study the key and chain. He wanted to apply the scientific method, make sure his hypothesis was correct.

The chain clinked as it tightened. He coughed. His black eyes began to bulge. He could not be killed. He was immortal. Regardless, the ever-tightening chain was becoming unbearable. Through his pain, he forced out a chuckle. The trick had become evident. He chuckled to spite God, to show him his torture was not working.

Clink, clink; the chain tightened further. He cried out a curse, the laughter falling away. It was the worst pain he had ever endured. If he were mortal, he would commit suicide to stop the pain. For him though, death could not be his escape. He had no choice. He had to unlock the chain. Anger filled him. He didn't want to use the key. That was just what the enemy wanted him to do. He would not be their puppet.

Clink, clink; he shrieked in agony. Determined to resist, he crumpled to the ground, screaming and writhing.

One more *clink.* The pain multiplied as his iron will shattered.

In rage and pain, he was barely aware of what he was doing. The key entered the keyhole. He turned it. The lock opened. The chain fell. The pressure released.

He gasped, rubbing his neck as he rose to his hands and knees. He hated this position, that of a wallowing animal. After a moment, after a deep breath, he rose to his feet. He felt much better now the chain had been removed. He felt no more pain, but there was something more. He realized the chain had been there around his neck for a very long time, invisible to him until just now. With the chain gone, everything changed.

He stood up, tall with a new level of pride. The desert sand no longer irritated him. He felt stronger than ever! *No,* he corrected himself. He had felt this strong once before. He remembered his strength in the days before his fall from heaven. He was among the strongest of angels then, and now that strength had returned.

He turned his back to the approaching expedition which he had been monitoring. They would be heading towards the egg. He would have to get there first. With a battle cry like thunder, he flew off towards the egg. The speed at which he traveled confirmed it. His power had truly been untethered. His battle cry echoed through the dunes, swelling in his elation. His time had arrived.

*

The expedition stopped dead in their tracks. Everyone in unison cocked their heads, listening. Moses was unsure what he'd heard. Thunder? Something else? Whatever it was, it conjured memories of that dark figure.

In the hot desert, Moses shivered. The chill that had entered him at sight of the figure now deepened. It was the chill of terror.

*

Lucifer did not have far to go. The egg was but a few dunes away. He arrived far ahead of the enemy, grateful for his new-found speed. He needed the time to prepare for them. He was back in battle-mode, strategizing. His objective was simple: protect the egg at all costs.

He smiled. In full power, this would be easy. Suddenly, his smile faded. A flicker of doubt lingered. A small voice in his head whispered, *it might still be a trick of some kind.*

No!" He pushed the doubt from him. "The scriptures do not lie." He turned to scan a gigantic hole in the sand. From where he stood, it appeared bottomless. He knew it was not. Deep within the hole, the bottom existed. And in its center, rested the egg. With the egg, his future also rested. Once it hatched, all Hell would break loose, metaphorically and literally.

He stared into that abyss. The moment of truth had arrived. If his power was truly untethered, he should have no trouble summoning his army for battle.

He closed his eyes. He bowed his head. He raised his hands. Things began to happen.

CHAPTER 11

Bob Gulam stood at the door of the bunker, the music from outside crashing against his brain. He nodded to the one who stood at attention, waiting for orders.

Upon his leader's nod, the woman typed in a code on the key-pad mounted beside the door. She hit the enter button and a LED screen above the door began a countdown. *30, 29, 28, 27...*

When it reached zero, Bob knew, all hell would break loose. *26, 25, 24, 23...*

Despite the stress, he smiled. What had he been thinking when he purchased the LED screen. How cheesy. The only thing separating this moment from an *Austin Powers* scene was the lack of a British accent intoning the numbers. The music throbbed. *22, 21, 20, 19...*

And, too—he was a far cry from Doctor Evil. He was not evil at all; he simply searched for truth in a world satisfied with myths. *18, 17, 16, 15...*

So what if he had to eliminate those who stood in the way of truth? He had to do what he had to do even if that meant going up against the most powerful government in the world.

14, 13, 12, 11...

He was doing nothing short of what his country's founding fathers had done. He was a modern day George Washington for Pete's sake, fighting a tyrannical, closed-minded government so future generations could experience greater freedoms. *10, 9, 8, 7...*

He turned from the screen to study his followers, his fellow patriots. Each and every one wore stone-cold faces. Every one of them completely committed to the cause.

He turned back to the door. It was almost go-time. *6, 5, 4, 3...*

He hefted his Uzi. With a flick of his finger, he released the safety. *2, 1, 0.*

The seal released with a hiss. The electric motor came to life with a hum. The door began to slide open. A sliver of light beamed through the ever-widening gap, along with the raucous blare of *Love Will Keep Us Together.* Apparently even those who surrounded the compound had grown tired of John Denver and crooning muppets. Bob smiled. He guessed neither the Captain, nor Tennille had written their little ditty for siege purposes. He put his finger on the trigger and prepared for the onslaught.

The irony of the song tempered his tension. *A love song for a battle? Please.* He doubted the government had any love for the Seekers, and they most certainly had no plans to keep them together. The door continued to open.

The music ceased and the stress snapped back full-force.

A static-ridden voice broke the momentary silence. "You are surrounded. Drop your weapons!"

Bob did not drop his weapon and his ears did not pick up the sound of any of his followers dropping theirs. They were united in their cause and would die for it if necessary.

The door continued to slowly open wider and wider. The moment of truth had arrived.

CHAPTER 12

Lucifer grinned as the sand around him began to churn. He laughed, standing on the edge of the great abyss, staring into vast emptiness as he summoned his army.

He remembered well the last time he had summoned his troops—seven of them he had been allowed, then. Only seven. That, however, was when his powers were tethered. Now he had no restrictions.

The wind howled as it rose from the abyss and shrouded Lucifer in a flurry of sand. He breathed it in. He exhaled it out. It was invigorating. Within the howling, he heard voices. They were evil and blasphemous and made him laugh with delight. They grew louder, overwhelming the gale. Louder and louder the voices grew to a crescendo of chaos.

Lucifer felt the air of insanity caress his spirit. He felt it, but knew he was not insane. *Drunk with power? Perhaps, but not insane.* He was above insanity. He was all-powerful. He was Lucifer, the new King of Kings and Lord of Lords. *There was another who claimed that title.* The thought entered his mind. It sustained his laughter. *Jesus was a fool.*

The blasphemous voices grew clearer. Shapes emerged within the storm, dark figures. The voices on the wind claimed their bodies. His army was forming.

The storm died away. The dust settled.

Lucifer looked around in delight. All the demons bowed before him, awaiting his orders. "Rise!" he shouted.

They rose.

The ecstasy of the moment was intoxicating. He wanted to dance and laugh until he could dance and laugh no more! He refrained. It would not be proper for the new King of Kings and Lord of Lords to behave in such a fashion, especially at such a solemn moment.

The last remnants of the storm fizzled out. The last flurries of dust disappeared. A stillness filled the void. Lucifer soaked in the silence. The moment commanded reverence, for posterity's sake if for no other. This, after all was a moment for the history books, a memory for all eternity.

"Do you hunger?" he murdered the silence with this question.

"Yes, Lord!" came his demons' reply.

"Good!" he shouted back. "Humanity's crop is ripe. The time to harvest has arrived."

"Yes, Lord Lucifer!"

"Still, we must move cautiously. This is our time to rule. We have one opportunity to claim our kingdom. It must be done correctly."

"Yes!" they shouted.

He walked out and among his troops as they stood at attention. He felt fear rising from them. It elated him. Fear was essential to power.

"I feel your fear," he acknowledged. "Obey me with all of your heart, and your fears will amount to nothing."

"Yes, Lord!"

"If, however, you fail me, your fears will not compare to the reality I will deal out to you! Do you understand?"

"Yes!"

"Do all of you understand?"

"Yes!" they shouted still louder.

"Good. First, we protect the egg. An enemy force is approaching. Their goal is to destroy it. We cannot allow that.

"Yes, Lord!"

Their wholehearted reply was his delight.

CHAPTER 13

The expedition pushed onward. Except for the occasional gust, the storm had dissipated.

Moses shivered in the heat. Increasingly, he felt the eyes of unseen watchers. He found himself constantly staring into the vastness before him, trying to see who watched. He saw nothing. Carl, his father, and the rest trudged along in utter silence. Moses could feel the low morale. It was a contagion he breathed and absorbed.

At length, Carl broke the silence. "According to the scout, the egg should be directly in front of us, three dunes away."

They climbed to the top of the first of the three, but saw only more of the same. The dunes rolled like waves on a vast ocean as they crested one after another after another, though the spray of sand carried on the wind was far worse than the spray of seawater at the beach. As they descended into the valley, Moses longed to be home in the great city where the sands did not blow.

He disliked the valleys more than the peaks. Although the sand blew less down in the valleys, it was here he felt the most vulnerable. It was here the feelings of being watched grew most intense. In their imaginary ship, they crested the second wave; one dune closer to their goal, one wave closer to the egg. Into the last valley they descended. Then up the final wave of sand, they rose.

Moses looked at his father. His dad's face was stone-serious and almost as pale as Carl's. Such a complexion was not natural for his dad. It made Moses wonder what was going through his father's mind. The thought worried him. This was not the first time his father had faced the beast. The last time, despite his father's special abilities, he had nearly been killed. This time, Moses thought, it should be much safer. For this time, it will not be the beast itself, but just its egg that needs to be destroyed.

Slowly, the expedition rounded the final crest. Moses got his first glimpse of the great abyss that sheltered the egg. He stopped, frozen, with the rest. It was far more than he had expected. The sight dashed his hopes. Terror tore into him. He felt unable to breath, dizzy. He felt a crushing, invisible pressure pushing into him.

The demon army that guarded the abyss far outnumbered that of the expedition, all of them ready for battle, their armor glistening against the day's light.

Their faces could not be seen, but if the battle helmets they wore was any indication of the grotesque beings beneath, their demonic origins could not be denied. The likenesses forged onto those helmets indicated pure evil.

From the eye-holes of every helmet, shone a pair of red orbs. They glowed with dead light that could only be kindled in Hell's deepest fires.

As terrifying as these were, it was the one at their head who struck Moses with the most terror. He wore no armor, no helmet. This was the one in black. There was no doubt. This figure had been no figment of his imagination either before when he had seen him on the dune or now as he felt the pressure of that stare crashing into him once again.

The dark one stared directly at Moses. More, he stared into him.

Moses felt exposed as the dark one looked through him, exposing him like some supernatural x-ray machine. His shivers grew into tremors; tremors of terror.

*

Lucifer inhaled deeply. He could taste their fright on his forked tongue. He loved it. It soothed him. It was intoxicating. Reluctantly, he refrained from doing more than sample this blissful cocktail. He didn't want to become drunk on their terror. There would be time soon for such indulgences, but now, he needed a clear mind so he could cherish this memory for all time.

Behind him stood his minions. He did not turn to make sure they were there. He didn't need to. He knew they were loyal and ready. Plus, they craved souls and would not abandon the chance at a meal such as this.

He looked over the herd of souls trembling before him and saw the one who had seen him before. A grin curled across his face as he stared past the physical to torment the spiritual.

The fear from this one was especially gourmet. He tasted it and sighed. It was going to be a challenge to not give into drunkenness, but he would try. He would try.

*

Moses felt ill. The dark man watched them with blacker than black eyes. It made him feel squirmy, as if worms had nested within him and the larvae had hatched. His terror built a leaning tower inside him, one that could collapse into panic at any second. He swallowed hard. He must keep it together.

"Moses," a voice called to him.

The dark one was calling him?

"Moses." The voice came again, fainter than before.

Moses shook his head and everything cleared. He had not noticed the extent to which he had drifted. Now he realized.

Disgusted, he cast aside the spell in which his mind had been soaking. He glared at the dark figure. That creature no longer had a hold of him. Defiantly he glared.

"Moses!" It was his father, running toward him. "We have to flee!" He grabbed his arm.

The rest of the expedition was scrambling in retreat. Judging by the footprints in the sand, his father had made a beeline back for him. Anger surged in Moses. He had been weak. He'd let this dark one penetrate his thoughts. He'd endangered his father's life with the need to rescue him.

Hunter scooped his son over his shoulder and raced after the others, counting, *counting! One—two—three—four—five*. Moses looked back as he was carried away. The demons looked on as if the expedition's retreat was a non-event. They did not pursue them—at least not yet.

*

Lucifer was elated, watching the little party run. They had fled in unison but for one. That one, he had captivated with his untethered power and then allowed him to break free: another piece of evidence his power was now absolute.

Now he had violated this one, he knew: they had met before, when this mortal was just an infant. Memories flooded his mind. This was the one he had planned to devour so long ago.

He frowned. This was the one who had escaped his grasp when the last beast had risen to power. This was the offspring of the ones who had defeated him the last time. His frown deepened. He would have his revenge. Not now, but soon.

He turned his head toward the door to the Space Between. The door had not been there a moment before. He wished it and it appeared before him.

With nothing more than a thought, the door widened. He stretched it. Such action was easy for him now that he had his unlimited strength. He stretched it until the opening gaped large enough for his army to pass through. He gave the command and those of his troops which he called, followed him through the door.

CHAPTER 14

"I repeat!" blared the voice of authority over the P.A. system. "Drop your weapons!"

Bob had no intention of dropping anything, especially not his weapon. The big door had now fully opened, giving him his first view of the enemy other than what he had seen on the television and security cameras. He tried to size them up but could not. One fact became evident. The Seekers were vastly outnumbered.

It didn't surprise him. *Leave it to Big Brother to be the bully,* he thought as he looked over those who dared to push into the Seeker's land. The firepower displayed by these invaders was far superior to their own. *One would think the Union was a band of terrorists for goodness sake.*

Upon a distant knoll, a chopper descended. *Rat-tat-tat.* The blades cut the air as it landed. More troops jumped out of the chopper. The Union was becoming a smaller minority with every passing moment. Despite the fear, which he tried to push away, he took a step forward. He walked beyond the threshold of the bunker, into the red zone.

"Drop your weapon!"

Bob did not respond to the command. Conversely, he made no attempt of overt aggression either. He knew enough about U.S. military procedure to know he stood the best chance of gaining time alive if he showed no aggression. After the fiasco at the Branch Davidian compound, the feds would be reluctant to draw first blood. They didn't need that kind of negative publicity, not again.

"It does not need to end this way!" the voice boomed.

Bob laughed to himself as he thought about the ludicrousness of that statement. Of course it had to end this way. How else could such a situation end?

He took another step forward and was warned again to stop. His heart pounded and his breathing quickened. He was challenging the most powerful government on Earth, and against the odds he was betting to win. *What a rush.*

"Stop where you are!"

He did not stop. He took another step forward. He didn't know how it was going to play out. He only knew it was indeed about to play out. He dangled his uzi from its shoulder strap, taking care to avoid aggressive moves. If he was perceived as an immediate threat, he'd soon have more holes than a brick of Swiss cheese. But whether he showed aggression or not was irrelevant. The enemy would lose patience with his non-compliance, even if it were done in a non-aggressive manner. It was only a matter of time.

That was what it was all about: time. He had the Ra on his side. He only needed to buy time for them to come to his aid. The three dice in his pocket had foretold his success. They had rolled the highest number and the dice did not lie.

He took another step and all Hell broke loose.

CHAPTER 15

Lucifer breathed in the ectoplasm that engulfed the Space Between. He filled his lungs with it and spewed it back out.

His chosen followers were close on his heels. He didn't need to look back to know they followed. They would follow him anywhere. They were his. Still, he turned to look—his army filled him with pride. He wanted to remember this moment forever, the moment he conquered the Earth.

He watched his dark demons fly through the space between. He could not see them in detail. The embryotic-like fluid through which they traveled blurred their features.

His speed increased. Like a magnet, the pull of his desired destination tugged at him. The further he traveled, the giddier he grew. He had waited from time beyond time for this moment. Even now, it seemed in some ways to be only a dream.

He pushed such doubts from him. The scriptures do not lie. They foretold these events. This was happening. This was real. He flexed his muscles as he flew, feeling power surge through him like snakes through a field of grass. Every yard brought him closer to Inner Earth. Every foot brought him one step closer to his great destiny.

He shouted the shout of a great warrior, but within the confines of the Space Between, it was muted. It didn't matter. With or without volume, the warrior's cry was genuine.

Ahead, the gloom of the Space Between gradually lightened. He was nearing his destination. He glanced behind, confirming he was traversing from comparative gloom to comparative brightness.

He smiled as he thought about the place to which he was headed. Inner Earth would soon be his. Conquering it would take some time, but it would succumb to his will sooner versus later, of this he was certain. He would need to strategize his conquest. It would be simple, he decided. He would sway souls away from the enemy using sugar instead of vinegar. Of course for those that did not like sugar, vinegar would be ready and waiting. For every soul that put their faith in him, the enemy would be that much weaker. Just as the angels in heaven celebrate every time a soul repents and is saved, so he rejoiced every time one was stolen away.

The seeds of his deception had already been planted. Splinter had already begun to perpetuate the lies among human kind. Even now, he had a group of followers, those who called themselves the Union of Seekers. Of course, these fools didn't understand they were following demons. Surely no one would follow demons willingly. No, he and his army would appear as the benevolent Ra, come to enlighten human kind and lead them to a higher state of evolution.

Lucifer knew they would buy into that little fairy tale easily enough. *How stupid of them.* He made a mental note to reward Splinter for his service. If all worked as planned, he would make Splinter a high-ranking General.

He exited the Space Between, spewing out the goo of that place, exchanging it for air. He had arrived!

The first thing he saw was two groups of armed men. They appeared ready to destroy each other. He flicked out his forked tongue, tasting the animosity flowing between the two groups. He loved the taste. It was wonderful.

*

Bob heard a sickening noise *rat-tat-tat* and knew the bullets had begun to fly. He hated the FBI. Apparently, they had learned nothing from the disaster at Waco. He dropped to the ground, minimizing himself as a target. He squeezed his own trigger, bringing the uzi to life. It spit out streams of hollow point lead.

He expected to die. It would be a martyr's death. But he refused to die alone. He chose instead to invite as many enemy soldiers as he could to join him in death. The invites were his shots fired, no need to RSVP. A crazy grin covered his face as the uzi vibrated with the repetitiveness it was designed for.

Strange thoughts entered his mind, thoughts of typewriters. Everything sounded like a busy office from the pre-computer age. Any second, the enemy's bullets would mow him down. A second passed, then another. He felt no pain. More seconds ticked by. He kept firing.

What's the delay? he wondered, regarding his own death. He should be worm-food by now. Everything moved so slowly. The gunfire, the war cries—it all took on a lethargic attitude. Bob had never been in a battle. He had no idea if such time-distortion was normal. It didn't feel normal. *Maybe I'm already dead,* he thought as he continued to squeeze the trigger. *Perhaps this is just a mirage my brain is projecting as it uses its last molecules of oxygen.*

He had heard of scientific studies about brain activity in the first seconds after physical death. He supposed it was possible he was already dead, but his brain was refusing to accept that reality, fabricating fiction before succumbing to the inevitable. In his delirium, he looked behind. His followers were there, firing weapons and shouting like savages. They moved as he did, in some strange time-delay atmosphere. He regarded them, expecting them to drop like flies exposed to insecticide. They did not drop dead. *How strange.*

He turned back to his enemy. He still fired his weapon, but nothing was coming from the barrel. The magazine was empty. He looked toward the FBI blockade. Surely they had casualties. He saw none. He was thinking about this conundrum when he saw something he had not noticed before. There was a haze in the air in front of him.

Bob's first thought was that the government had deployed some kind of chemical weapon, mustard gas maybe. He quickly dismissed the idea. First, the haze didn't seem to have any negative affect. Second, it seemed as much among the enemy troops as among the Union of Seekers.

The more he observed it, the less he thought of it as a haze at all. It was more of a darkness. He could see the Feds, but it was like looking at them through a plague of locusts frozen in time and space.

Suddenly, his brain made an identification. He realized what it was. It was not a swarm of locusts, but a swarm of bullets! Every round that had been fired from either side was suspended in the space between the two factions. They had no forward momentum, yet they did not fall.

Bob looked up from the haze. He saw that which he assumed was holding the bullets in place. Bob struggled to his feet, a gleeful smile on his face. The Ra had arrived!

CHAPTER 16

Lucifer, in his untethered state had stopped the two opposing factions from destroying each other. He did it not out of the goodness of his heart, but to secure his earthly throne. With his hands raised, he supported countless bits of lead and wartime ordinance. They hung there, suspended in the air, waiting on his commands.

With a flick of his wrists, he sent them into motion. Under his control, they swarmed into a vortex, a deadly tornado.

"Splinter!" Lucifer shouted.

"Yes, Lord!" Splinter immediately answered.

"Go speak your truth to the ones who know you." He smiled. 'Truth' from a master-fibber like Splinter was not truth at all but lies disguised to sound like honesty.

"Yes, Lord," Splinter said as he went.

*

Splinter was thankful his master had given him permission to depart. His demonic heart had crumbled with fear when Lucifer called him. One never knew what Lucifer's summons meant, after all. It could be a call to punishment, and punishment by Lucifer was unbearable.

Splinter levitated around the swirling vortex of death, moving toward the Union of Seekers, toward Bob Gulam. He thought of all the wonderful lies he would weave. He smiled. Lies were his milieu, the medium he used as a sculptor would clay, or a dancer, music, to determine their sway. He drew near to the First Seeker. He extended his hands to him, palms out. He would be perceived as one coming in peace. *Ah, the first lie, how delicious.*

*

Bob saw Splinter coming. Relief permeated his entire being. Every cell within him had been tense from battle. Now, he relaxed. He had forced himself to rely on the prophecy from his dice. He knew deep down the Ra would not abandon the Seekers, and indeed they hadn't. They had proved themselves to him once again. They were the true gods, here to support those who believed in them. And now the Seekers had put their lives on the line in the name of truth, and the Ra had come to save them.

As Splinter approached, Bob tried to take in as much detail as he could. He wanted to remember this moment as long as he lived. But his eyes flickered past Splinter, toward the leader. He wore black, had short cropped darker than dark hair and pale-white skin. These traits were unremarkable compared to his eyes. Those eyes had the air of authority and they drew Bob to him. More accurately, they drew Bob into him.

The leader's eyes met Bob's, locked into a symbiotic stare, for just a moment. Bob had to look away. Those eyes were too intense, too dark, like looking into the infinity of a black hole. Even looking away, he could sense those eyes as they looked into him and through him; surrounding him like a flame surrounds a dry leaf.

He lifted his eyes back to Splinter. He could look at Splinter—maybe because they had met before. He knew one thing. This day would be one for the history books. Henceforth, this day would be known as *Seeker's Salvation Day.*

CHAPTER 17

Alice held her baby tight as she watched the news on the hotel room's television. Her husband Adam sat beside her. Their eyes were glued to that screen, their faces aghast.

For days now, the media had been covering what had been dubbed *The Oregon Waco Siege*. By all accounts, this was the news story of the century, a reporter's dream. For her, this was not a dream at all. It was a nightmare.

"There he is!" Alice shouted as she pointed at the screen. Her finger shook as she pointed. "Now do you believe me?" Her voice was shrill. "There he is, just like I described him."

She had a swirl of fright and relief bottled up inside her. The fright came from knowing she had met this dark one before and she knew who he was. The relief was having proof she was not crazy. Lucifer existed.

She looked at her husband. He continued to stare at the screen. His complexion was pale. His face was altogether indescribable. She knew Adam believed everything she had told him. How could he not believe really, after everything he had been through, with their home burning to the ground and those who had attacked him just prior to torching their place. Lucifer's goons had meant Adam to die in the flames that day, but God had other plans. His life had been spared, though the fire had left them nowhere to go but a hotel. Yes, she knew he believed everything that had happened. Still, it was good to have proof.

That proof now stared out at her from the TV. She had described to Adam in as much detail as she could, what the leader of demons looked like. Now he was right there on the idiot box, she knew her description of him did not do justice. He appeared more powerful and more dangerous and far more evil than she remembered.

The thermostat in the room was set at a comfortable 76 degrees, yet she shivered as she watched the prince of demons in high definition resolution. Icy claws of fear grasped at her. On the television, the Devil hovered in mid-air, a swarm of bullets and military ordinance floating about and around him. The scene looked like something from a Hollywood special effects shop, but she knew it was no illusion. It was real and that knowledge chilled her further.

Whoever was in charge of the camera work must have realized the extreme importance of what was happening. He zoomed in, a close-up straight from Hell. Black, soulless eyes stared out from the flat-screen. Alice knew Lucifer was only looking into a camera, yet she felt as if he were looking at her directly, searching for her specifically. She began to sob.

Adam put his arms around her and pulled her close. That was one of the things she had always loved about him, his strength. She needed that strength even though she suspected it was only a facade. She could feel his trembling as he held her. It gave him away.

The eyes glared out at her. She suddenly felt sick and turned away from it. Still, in her mind, she saw those black soulless eyes; searching, watching. She felt her husband's arm on her shoulder as she wept. "Adam, I don't believe it myself, but it's him. It's him and I know why he's here. He's come to take our baby! He wants Kerry!"

"I believe you," Adam responded without hesitation.

She looked into his eyes and despite the situation, she cracked a thin smile. She was glad he believed her. She needed that.

After a moment, he spoke. "I think we need to disappear for a while."

She nodded her agreement. "And Pastor Garrett needs to come with us."

Pastor Garrett was the only other person who knew the truth about little Kerry and how the Devil had a hit out on the child. Within minutes, they had the diaper bag loaded and had left the hotel room. They didn't bother to turn off the television, nor did they bother to check out. They simply fled.

CHAPTER 18

Seeker's Salvation Day - plus three days.

*

Bob stood in a far corner of the room. In the opposite corner Splinter conversed with the Ra leader referred to as Lucifer. Bob had been summoned and he didn't know why. So much had happened in the last three days. It was hard to keep track. The Ra had come just in the nick of time and saved the Seekers from certain annihilation. It was clear the Seekers had a debt to repay. His thoughts came back to the present. The world was in a strange state of quiet awe, on the brink of something big.

Bob shook his head. With the exception of those in the Union of Seekers, the inhabitants of this planet didn't understand the truth that had come to them. Even the Seekers didn't have all the answers, but he had the feeling that soon, many more would come to know what the Union knew and so much more.

He stared at Lucifer from the far side of the room. Even though the Ra leader had saved them from certain death, he felt uncomfortable near him. Bob couldn't explain why, but he felt unsteady in the worst way whenever this dark one drew close. Such was the case now as he stood opposite Lucifer. He wanted to be comfortable around their savior, but it wasn't happening, at least not yet. He hoped that with time, his feelings would change.

Concluding his conversation, Lucifer turned and looked directly at Bob. Bob's mouth went dry. The black eyes stared out from the unnaturally pale face in a most peculiar manner. Such examinations left him feeling dirty and used. He tried to look back into those coal-black eyes. He failed. Something about them disallowed staring back. He dropped his gaze, like a dog who has been scolded by its owner. He stared at the ground until the unsettling feeling left. When he looked up, Lucifer was gone. Only Splinter remained.

"Where did he go?" Bob asked. He was surprised to hear such timidity in his voice.

"I don't know," Splinter answered him. "Lucifer answers to no one. He comes and goes as he pleases."

Despite Splinter's cryptic words, Bob understood this concept of rank. Lucifer was at the pinnacle of the pyramid, all others were beneath him. Where in this pyramid did he fit, he wondered. The answer eluded and worried him.

"Do you have a tattoo artist among you?" Splinter inquired.

Bob nodded. "We do."

"Summon him. His skills will soon be needed."

Bob wanted to say more, but Splinter had exited the room. Bob hoped it would be okay that the tattoo artist was not a male, but a female. The Ra did not strike him as a sexist bunch; they appeared to be more equal opportunity intimidators. His head swam with this new request. What did the Ra want with a tattoo artist? He smiled despite himself as he pictured the Ra all inked up. The image didn't fit them.

JoAnne, he thought. *I need to track down JoAnne.*

*

He found JoAnne in the main bunker. She was not easy to miss with her neon pink Mohawk and skin covered in tribal art patterns. She had done many of her tattoos herself, which Bob had heard is not easy. This ability to focus while in pain had impressed him early on in their relationship.

He roved his eyes over every inch of her exposed flesh. Her art was exquisite. She had a skill beyond what could be taught. It was a natural-born talent, ingrained in her very DNA. It was a skill that was now needed.

JoAnne was wearing a camouflage-print sports bra and matching fatigue pants. The cuffs of her pants were tucked into combat boots. JoAnne had been one of the more recent converts to the Seekers. He did not fully trust her. He had nothing against her; she simply had not been there long enough to have earned his trust.

He approached. She looked up from the magazine she read as she sat on the floor with her back against the wall. The title was clearly printed on the cover: *Skin Ink*. The cover included a bikini-clad model displaying her tattoos in a most provocative fashion. Laying on the ground beside JoAnne was a Union-owned 38 and a box of shells. It was time to see if she could earn his trust.

CHAPTER 19

The family of three, Alice, Adam, and Kerry, was now four. Three days ago, they had knocked on Pastor Garrett's apartment door. He had opened it cautiously, keeping the security chain engaged. He had peeked out at them through that crack with fear evident on his face.

Alice knew that look. It had been one she herself had worn too often as of late. He knew what they knew. How could he not? The media was all over the story like white on rice. All regularly scheduled television and radio programming had ceased. Now only the progressing drama of the new arrivals aired in a perpetual 24 hour rotation. According to media reports, the newcomers called themselves the Ra and they had come to enlighten those earthlings who chose to believe in them. Alice knew the truth. The Ra was a ruse to hide their true identity. They were demons.

Once Garrett was sure his friends had not been followed, he released the security chain. He ushered them in quickly, locking the door behind them with the jittery movements of an insect on crack cocaine. Now he, like they, had abandoned the life he had once lived to flee the coming calamity they felt certain was about to be unleashed.

Garrett was still recovering from his last encounter with Lucifer. His bruises were still healing and he still wore his left arm in a sling from when it had so cruelly been wrenched out of socket. So they fled. They did not know where they were fleeing to, they simply fled.

Their first stop had been the bank where Alice and Adam had their accounts. They cashed them out, requesting nothing larger than twenties. The next stop had been Garrett's bank. He did the same thing. Cash was impersonal and hard to connect with the user. They couldn't use plastic, for fear they could be tracked.

They smashed their cell phones and another traceable element of their lives were gone.

The next step was new transportation. Adam and Alice had no idea how to get a non-trackable car. Garrett had surprising connections, however, for a man of the cloth. They took his Dodge Durango, left the familiarity of their section of town, and entered the inner-city.

CHAPTER 20

Run! Run! RUN! This was the repetitive shouts that screamed inside of Moses' head as he fled from the demon-riddled abyss. In his mind, the one with the blacker than black eyes pursued him. Being carried by his father, he quickly passed all of the others who were fleeing.

He was grateful his father had rescued him. But he felt foolish being the one who had become mesmerized by the dark-eyed one and needed rescuing. Plus, being carried made him feel like a child. His foolishness mixed with guilt. When he had first seen the dark figure on the dune, he should have said something. He hadn't and now it was too late to fix that mistake.

He glanced back, expecting demonic fingers reaching for him. He saw nothing of the sort. His father must have realized they were not being pursued because he slowed to a jog. One by one, the other expedition members slowed and stopped, spread out over the expanse of a wide valley between two great dunes. Each of them now stood as still as statues, waiting for any change. Moses felt his pounding heart as it thumped in his chest. Nothing else stirred. They had been left alone—at least for the moment.

CHAPTER 21

A strange feeling nagged at JoAnne as Bob escorted her to the designated meeting place. Of course she would feel strange, she thought. She was about to meet the leader of an entire alien race.

She thought of that leader and the feeling morphed into fear. Although she was a member of the Union of Seekers and now adhered to that philosophy, she had been raised in a Christian house. The name Lucifer was not unknown to her.

Regardless, she did not understand why that name still held such disdain. She was no longer a Christian. She no longer believed in that God or in the existence of a devil. She tried to rationalize this, but the name of the biblical prince of darkness still sent shivers down her spine. She couldn't help it.

As she allowed herself to be escorted along, she thought back to her first meeting with Bob Gulam. It had been two years since he had shown her the way to true enlightenment. So far, her faith in the Union had paid off. Now the Ra had arrived and the promised enlightenment had been offered. She felt lucky to be in that number.

She entered the room where the meeting was to take place. Her knees grew weak as the door shut behind her with a sound of finality. She turned back. Bob was not there. Apparently, he was not to be a part of this meeting. Dizziness overwhelmed her. She turned from the door.

There was Lucifer.

He stood at the far end of the room, motionless. She stared at him —at his pale skin and black hair. The room seemed to disappear. It was just the two of them, intimate and alone; surrounded by an indescribable darkness.

Lucifer shifted and everything came back into focus. JoAnne's knees gave out. She stayed upright only by using the nearby wall for support. She could feel him looking not at her, but into her, examining her from the inside out. She swallowed hard. She wanted to scream. She swallowed again, feeling the need to keep quiet in the presence of this royalty.

"Do not fear me," he commanded her.

She nodded and tried to obey but found such obedience impossible. She *did* fear, and it was a fear that went deeper than the sound of his name or its significance from her Christian past. It was the fear she had lost control of her own destiny, that her life was no longer her own.

He continued to stare, violating her with his eyes.

Her discomfort bordered on pain.

"I am told you possess a great talent." He smiled. It wasn't a pleasant smile.

JoAnne didn't answer. She couldn't find the words.

"I speak of your skill as an artist."

She managed a nod.

"I have a very special job for you."

Strangely, his approval of her skills filled her with emotion. It was not joy she felt, but something akin to relief. Despite his approval, she still could not look at him directly. Those black eyes of his were too intense.

"Do you have the tools of your trade with you?"

She heard him ask as if he were speaking to her from the far end of a long tunnel. She nodded. No self-respecting tattoo artist ever went anywhere without their kit.

"Good. Bring your tools here. Your job must begin immediately."

CHAPTER 22

They had accomplished what they needed to and were now leaving the inner-city. Alice felt good about driving away. Even more so, she felt fortunate that Pastor Garrett was with them.

Never in a million years would she have suspected that goody-two-shoes Garrett would have such connections—connections she classified as seedy at best.

Before he took over her church, Garrett had worked with troubled inner-city youth. As a result, he knew where to go to discretely get rid of his Durango. They traded it straight up plus two hundred dollars for a hot, midnight-blue Nissan Rogue. By hot, those that sold the car did not mean its temperature or spice level. The Nissan was stolen and came with counterfeit plates.

Garrett put the two hundred bucks in his pocket prior to meeting with his connections. It would be wise, he warned Alice and Adam, not to let these people know how much cash they were toting around.

They handed over the keys to the Durango and received in return, a modified screwdriver to start the Nissan. With a twist of the screwdriver's handle into the tampered-with ignition, the car came to life. Alice glanced at the Dodge one last time as they drove away. Soon, it would enter the chop shop and cease to exist except as spare, and untraceable, parts. Parting ways from the vehicle did Alice good. She had bad memories associated with it.

Under any other circumstances, Alice would not feel comfortable with the decisions they were making. She had never so much as stolen a stick of gum, and now she was riding in a stolen vehicle with counterfeit plates. She sighed and forced the thoughts from her mind. This was a crime of necessity, for self-preservation. The Devil himself was after them for goodness sake.

Garrett drove, with Adam beside him in the front passenger seat. Alice got as comfortable as she could in the back. Beside her, Kerry slept peacefully in her car seat.

Adam huffed as he turned on the radio. "I'm afraid to hear what this is going to tell us." He tuned into a station that was normally all music. It hadn't played music in days.

A voice came over the airwaves. "And so the promise is about to be made. I have been told the leader of the Ra will speak shortly. We have not been told specifics on when exactly, but soon. Do stay tuned to this station for further developments." The station reverted to stories recorded earlier reminiscing about all that had happened up to that point.

Alice's heart sank. She hated listening to the news. But she had no choice. They would need to keep up on any developments. Their lives depended on it.   She felt as if she was falling from a plane without a parachute. She bit her lip in anticipation of the fast-approaching collision.

CHAPTER 23

Without delay, JoAnne retrieved her kit. She dared not dillydally. She had the impression Lucifer didn't tolerate such things. She peered through the open doorway, reluctant to enter. There stood Bob Gulam and Lucifer. They stood close, conversing in whispers at the far end of the room. Pushing past her reluctance, she entered.

The two stopped whispering, leaving in their wake, a void of silence. The only noise she heard came from herself. Her own breathing boomed like a great bellows. Her beating heart sounded like war drums. Her flowing blood sounded like Colorado rapids racing down a steep ravine. Her thoughts shrieked.

Bob and Lucifer stared at her. She felt the weight of their stares. Bob's didn't bother her much. Lucifer's however, was crushing. His dark eyes once again roved over and through her like a living X-ray machine designed to see through more than flesh and expose much more than bones. She knew she had to please this one. Whatever it was he wanted from her, she had to do it. Success was her friend, and failure her mortal enemy.

"Did you bring your tools?" Lucifer broke the silence like a sledgehammer crashing upon fine crystal.

She nodded. His voice penetrated her ears and sent shivers down her spine, repulsive shivers. She held up her briefcase which held her tattoo gun, inks, and other pieces of equipment essential to her trade.

"Good. Let me present to you your first customer." With a dramatic gesture, he indicated Bob Gulam.

She inched closer. Repulsion built with every step. She wanted to turn tail and run, but knew such actions would be pointless. She was in far too deep for such a simple solution. Plus, she had the feeling she had nowhere to run.

Bob took a seat in a nearby recliner and put up the footrest. Lucifer took a step back and ushered her to her new client.

"What do you want me to do?" She tried to be bold, but her voice sounded weak.

Lucifer answered with the boldness she lacked. "Tattoo him. That is what you do, is it not?"

His voice remained benign, but JoAnne felt the presence of a malignancy hidden in that calm. She would need to tread lightly. She did not want to reap the whirlwind.

Bob held out to her his right hand, palm up. "I want you to tattoo me here."

"And when you are finished there," Lucifer said, "do the same tattoo there." He indicated Bob's forehead.

She nodded.

"And when you are done with him, do the same to all of the Seekers including yourself."

"And then to all those who join in the future," Bob added.

Lucifer nodded. "Yes. Together we will form a new order, for the old has passed away and is no more."

JoAnne was not excited. She was an artist, not an assembly-line factory worker. She had no desire to do the same tat over and over again. She said nothing however. She would not cross the Ra.

"I'll need much more ink," she said. It was the best excuse she could muster. The excuse fell flat.

"You will not use your own ink. The Ra will provide it all."

As he spoke, he produced a container of ink that appeared to be compatible with her equipment. He handed it to her. She took it.

It felt icy cold in her palm. Rather than the heat of her hand warming it, it seemed to leach all of the heat from her.

She stared at Bob's open right hand. "What do you want me to tattoo?"

Lucifer answered her and what he told her was disturbing, but she was in far too deep to decline. She had run out of options. In fear, she began her work.

CHAPTER 24

Lucifer exited through the main entrance of the bunker. Immediately the media circus died down. The hum of a mosquito, at that moment, would have sounded like a sonic boom. He approached the podium and looked over the crowd. The silence itself seemed to squirm under the pressure of the moment, a worm under a descending foot.

"Citizens of Earth," he began the deception. "No doubt you feel you have been left in the dark. Understandably, you have many questions. I will attempt to shed some light." Lucifer smiled at his choice of words. The light he shone would only create more darkness in men.

*

I am Lucifer, Leader of the Ra. And who is the Ra, you may be asking yourselves? We are a race of universal travelers. We explore. We experiment. We are your gods in the sense that we created you.

Back when this planet had cooled enough to support life, we planted the seeds of life and watched it grow. Life is like anything. It starts out small and primitive and slowly evolves into more complex entities. It's a universal rule. Some of what evolved was due to natural selection. Others was the result of our direct intervention.

Of all the life on this planet, we are simultaneously most satisfied and frustrated with humans. At the dawn of human evolution, there was a common primate ancestor. It was an animal, nothing more, but we *made* it something more.

We injected it with our own DNA, the spark of the gods. The primate became greater than it had been. It became human and capable of producing more humans in our image.

Over the course of many generations, you grew and learned how to harness your intelligence. Despite your intelligence however, you had flaws. It was in your nature to glorify things. You began to see us as gods, demons, spirits, and the like.

Because of this, we left you; preferring to observe you from a distance. It was not right for you to make us something we were not. We hoped that in our absence, you would begin to move past such primitive beliefs.

In more recent times, you have begun to evolve past your obsession with religion and gods and goddesses. Thanks to the Union of Seekers, we have finally felt it was time to return and make ourselves known.

So, now the Ra has returned, we make this proclamation: The time has arrived to cleanse the human race and become what we made you to be. Believe in us and we will enlighten you. Believe in us and you will become more than you were.

*

With that, he concluded. He left the podium in silence and with a smile. By proclaiming what would become of those who put their faith in the Ra, he opened a question in their minds. Each of them was now wondering what might become of those who refused to follow the Ra. He would let that question simmer in their brains. He would 'enlighten' them more at a later time, but for now his job was done. Mankind would follow him, he was sure of it.

CHAPTER 25

Having turned off the radio in disgust, they drove on in silence. Garrett couldn't believe what had been delivered to him via the Nissan's radio.

They were on the interstate now, the city far behind. His arm ached. It must have been time for some of his prescription pain killers. He hoped he wouldn't need the pills much longer as he doubted he could get a prescription refill without revealing their location and identity. He drove with his knees, popped the cap off of the amber medicine bottle with his good hand, and dry-swallowed two pills.

His life had changed in a very short time. Just days ago, he had been the pastor at Holy Trinity church. Now, he was a fugitive from evil. He glanced in the rear view. As far as he could see, they weren't being followed. He compulsively glanced again. Still no one. He would have to get used to this new life of always looking over his shoulder. There was no going back to the way things had been.

He looked into the mirror a third time and caught a glance of Alice and little Kerry in the rear seat. It hit him then and there. God had called him to be more than just a fugitive from demons. He was also called to protect this young family.

He didn't understand why, but he knew the demons coveted Kerry for their own demented purposes. He felt deeply that this baby held some importance in the overall scheme of things. He must ensure the demons never got their scaly hands on her. He would keep her safe at all costs.

They drove south. The final destination, he didn't know. South just felt right. He worried not only for himself and those with him, but for all of mankind. Over the generations, man had lost touch with God. Even during his lifetime, he had witnessed a general fading of faith in Jesus as the one who held the power to save. Sure, there were still those to be found who remained loyal to Christ, but nothing more than a remnant of what had once been.

And now, the Ra had arrived. He feared this would be the final nail in the coffin for many. The Ra was a new kind of idol, more dangerous than all the others combined. The Ra were not who they claimed to be—he knew from experience. They were demons and their leader Satan himself.

Garrett was shocked at the Devil's boldness. He was weaving a lie into the world, without even bothering to hide his name. The world knew him as Lucifer, yet seemed blinded to the identity associated with that name. Such boldness chilled Garrett. A tear strolled down his cheek as he thought about the path mankind was about to venture on.

The thought enticed him to speed up. Wherever they were headed, he wanted to get there as quickly as possible. He pushed down on the gas pedal, driving them south. He still was not sure why south—he just knew they had to escape the encroaching evil.

He glanced in the rear view once more. Alice had dozed off, but Kerry had woken up. He could see the child's dark brown eyes glimmering. They were such pretty eyes, such unusual eyes. *I will protect you,* he thought as he looked at those eyes via the rear view reflection. *With God as my witness, I will protect you.*

CHAPTER 26

"And he causeth all, both small and great, rich and poor, free and bond, to receive a mark in their right hand, or in their foreheads." – Revelation 13:16

*

Repulsion filled JoAnne as she finished her work on Bob. It surprised her. She was no amateur and had been doing her art for years. She had never turned down a client no matter how disturbing the tattoos they wanted. As long as they paid her, she was their artist. Moreover, Bob's tattoo was not repulsive in appearance. So, by process of elimination, she figured her repulsion was a combination of the ink used and the meaning behind the image.

She stood back from her work as she always did with clients when she finished. She liked to see a more distant perspective just to make sure everything looked right. In this case, nothing looked right. The art was flawless, but her repulsion doubled as she viewed both the image on Bob's right hand and the identical one on his forehead at the same time.

"What's wrong?" Bob inquired.

She hesitated to answer. The Ra were the new unquestioned leaders. Bob was loyal to them. She wasn't sure how he would respond if she voiced her repulsion of their marks. "Nothing's wrong."

"You look like you're ready to puke your guts out."

"No, I'm fine, really I am," she said, trying to compose herself.

Bob's eyes narrowed.

She wondered if he knew what she was trying to hide. Perhaps he was feeling the same. After all, it was his skin that now housed the Ra's ink.

"This represents us now. We are the first of the new order."

"The Union of Seekers," she said.

"No," he answered quickly. "That was the old order. From now on, we belong to the Union of the Ra."

She nodded. She wasn't sure she wanted to be a member of that union, not with that feeling of repulsion flowing through her veins.

"Along with the old order, perished our old symbol." He pitched his three dice from him. "My new tattoos are the new symbols. They're a union of the old dice and the new order. When you get your tattoos, you'll discard your dice as well."

She wasn't sure she wanted new tattoos. But she didn't see a way out of it.

"I know you do your own tattoos."

She nodded.

"I also noticed you do your work left-handed."

This was true. She didn't like where she saw the discussion headed.

He handed her a mirror. "It would be an honor to watch you do your forehead and your right palm."

"You would be honored?" She didn't think Bob had such sentiments.

"Not me, you. You will have the honor of becoming the second to be marked into the new order; by your own hand no less."

She took another step back. Her mind swam. She didn't want to tattoo herself with this alien ink. Her first instinct was to say there was no room. She was already covered with tattoos. Ironically though, her right palm and forehead was still available for ink.

Bob rested his hand on the handle of a pistol that stuck out of his waistband. She couldn't tell if the action was meant to threaten, but it did. "It's your turn, JoAnne." His fingers crawled over the wooden pistol-grip like a spider with a penchant for shooting practice. He thrust the mirror into her right hand. "Do your forehead first. I want to watch."

JoAnne felt a little bit of vomit sting the back of her throat. She took the mirror. She began to work. She began to cry as a part of her died inside.

CHAPTER 27

"And it shall come to pass afterward, that I will pour out my spirit upon all flesh; and your sons and daughters will prophesy. Your old men will dream dreams, your young men shall see visions." – Joel 2:28.

*

Matthew sat straight up, damp with sweat as were his sheets. He turned to his wife's side of the bed, but she was not there. *Where was she?* It took a few seconds for him to wake up fully. Then the memories hit and the sadness crept in. She had passed away more than two years ago. Memories of the funeral haunted him still. He would remember it in exquisite detail for the rest of his life.

He remembered the flowers on her casket down to the last petal; the mourner's sympathetic expressions and statements; the hot, dry day of her burial. It wasn't long after that the recurring dreams began, always the same, coming to him in black and white, like a pre-color-era movie. Usually, his dreams were vibrant with color, but not in this case. The lack of color must have importance. At least that was his thought.

In the dream, a small SUV careened down a desert road. Although it appeared black, he believed it was a dark color, maybe a deep blue. He didn't know why he thought that, when no blue was seen. That was simply the nature of the dream.

The SUV careened down the road with a rooster-tail of desert dust pluming up in its wake as if the road was a canal and the vehicle, a speedboat moving at top velocity, far past what was safe and probably even what was possible.

Despite the speed, he could see every detail, down to the features of those who rode inside. There were four of them. The driver wore a clerical collar and had one arm in a sling. The front passenger was a young man, somewhat younger than the driver, who looked to be in his mid to late twenties. In the back was a woman, also in her twenties.

What drew his attention most was the one beside the woman in an infant's car seat. In the dream, he could zoom in for the close-up image. The baby's eyes were always his focus. They were dark, very dark. In this colorless environment he couldn't tell where pupils began and irises ceased. They appeared as black holes surrounded by the whites of those eyes.

In this reoccurring dream, after zooming in on those eyes, his view always panned out from the occupants of the SUV to that which they were fleeing from. Darkness pursued them. Like a great dust storm, it consumed everything, throwing the land into blackness as it advanced.

The SUV flew like a rocket. But was it fast enough? Matthew could not tell. For the darkness was also fast. The darkness scared him. He sensed evil in it. He did not want those fleeing it to be consumed within. He feared what would happen when the gas ran out or the tires failed or the engine blew.

The answers to those questions remained unanswered as Matthew witnessed the chase. The car flew past the sign welcoming newcomers to Geddon, California. Matthew knew this town well. It was his home.

Geddon was a place you might miss if you blinked while driving through. But few people drove through it at all unless they knew where to find it. Geddon was a dying village in the southern California desert. It was not significant enough to get a dot on any known map and was never officially recognized as a community. This was the way the town had always been and this was the way the citizens of Geddon liked it. Anonymity was their friend.

The entire place consisted of a few dilapidated homes, a gas station, and a bar. There was no school. There was no post office. For the most part, the town was inhabited by loners who kept to themselves.

For this reason, it struck Matthew as odd that the SUV's occupants were in such a hurry to arrive in town. He wondered about the darkness that chased them—and what would happen if the darkness consumed Geddon.

He never wondered for long on this. It was always at this point that he woke up. Every time was the same. He woke up with the acrid smell of his own perspiration hanging on the air. He always looked first for his wife. Then he would remember the funeral and the truth, and a deep lonely sadness would invade him.

This time was no different. She was not there to comfort him just as she had not been for over two years now. He cried. He cried until he could do so no more.

CHAPTER 28

Bob approached the podium. His thoughts trailed back to the day he'd killed the reporter who had sneaked into the Union of Seekers' meeting. It wasn't so long ago but seemed to be lifetimes in his past.

He looked over the crowd. The crowd stretched as far as the eye could see. Many were from the media. *How ironic,* he thought. *Bob, killer of reporters, now drew them to himself like flies to a rotting carcass.* He scanned the media frenzy, then looked at his new master.

Lucifer smiled and nodded. Bob looked at his right palm, at the mark that showed his new allegiance. He understood why two tattoos were required. The one on his right hand reminded *him* to whom his allegiance belonged. The one on his forehead told the world.

A hush settled over the mob. He looked them over sternly. He didn't want to show any hint of weakness, not with them.

He announced Lucifer, and welcomed him to the podium. Then he stood back and took his rightful place as a distant second. Lucifer stood before the crowd and the crowd quieted. It was a silence so supreme that it bordered on madness.

*

Lucifer was pleased as he approached the microphone. This was the media. These were the messengers that would bring his message to the masses. Through them, he would perpetuate his lies.

"Earthlings," he began. "The Ra has returned."

He waited. Man was a bit slow and he wanted that first lie to stick in their brains. If it didn't, whatever he said after would be of little value.

"We have returned to enlighten those who choose to be enlightened."

He paused again. He waited. He continued. "In the past, you were allowed to follow anything you perceived as 'truth.' For some of you, that meant Christ. For others, it meant Buddha. For still others, the Great Spirit, or Mother Earth."

Another pause. He needed this next lie to really hit home. "It's all the same to the Ra. Christian, Buddhist, Muslim, or anything else; it's all false truths."

The stunned silence of the crowd encouraged him. They were swallowing his lies. He smiled. He continued. "That you are so zealous in seeking the truth is encouraging. However it saddens us that as a species, you are so easily misguided. So, we have come back to guide those who wish to be led."

Yet another pause. Then, his voice rising, he called out, "I proclaim this truth here and now: *There is no god but us*. We created you. We watched you develop as a species. You are our children."

Even though he smiled, he kept the hint of sternness in his eyes and made sure the cameras had the opportunity to get a good close-up. They must feel they had no choice but to listen and obey.

His voice boomed the next words. "Now is the time to give up your preconceived notions of what truth is or what god is. For now on, put your faith in us. We will enlighten you. Put your allegiance in us and we will be your providers. Put your loyalties with us, and it will go well with you."

He stopped short of saying what would happen if they did not follow the Ra. He would let them come to their own conclusions on that. He looked into the crowd. Their faces showed fear. He breathed in their fear. It was intoxicating. He loved it.

"You are my messengers. Tell the world what I have told you today. All who choose to follow this path of truth must receive the mark of the Ra. We come to you open armed. Now come to us and we will take you under our wings."

*

With that, he ended his speech. There would be more speeches to come, but for now he had told them enough. He wanted them to have time to contemplate these lies, time for their fears to germinate and grow.

He wanted them to believe.

The world would soon flock to him. He had woven his lies thoroughly. It was only a matter of time. He left them to stew in the broth of falsities in which he had bathed them. He left them to absorb his story.

CHAPTER 29

"Satan himself is transformed into an angel of light." – 2 Corinthians 11:14

*

Garrett slept, but it was not the sound sleep his body needed. His arm ached. The doctors had said it would for a while. But his injuries went deeper than the physical. The psychological scars would be there for life. Memories of his demonic battles remained.

He had the feeling the Devil and his minions had grown more powerful. The lies coming over the airways scared him. The Ra claimed they came as gracious benefactors.

Garrett saw through the lies. Most did not. Demons were trying to pull mankind away from the truth of Jesus, and down a path to their destruction. Despite his knowledge, there was so much he didn't understand—for instance, why the Devil wanted to murder little Kerry? What role did she play in his scheme? Whatever the reason, Lucifer had a price on Kerry's head. Garrett couldn't allow her to be caught. He opened his eyes. They burned with fatigue. The sun had not yet risen.

"Did you get some good sleep?" Adam asked as he drove the Nissan.

"Sure," Garrett lied.

"Good. Maybe in the next town we can trade off if you're up to it."

Garrett nodded. He turned to check the occupants of the back seat. Both Alice and Kerry slept. He wondered if their slumber was as fitful as his had been. He hoped not. They needed their rest. He turned back around. They passed a sign—not an official highway sign, but a homemade plywood banner. In reflective spray-paint letters, it announced a town up ahead that Garrett had never heard of. Its name was Geddon, California.

CHAPTER 30

Matthew couldn't sleep. This wasn't unusual. After waking from 'the dream' he often became restless. He got out of bed and walked to his front window, the one that faced the single road through the middle of Geddon. At this time of early morning, the deserted road was the norm. Not that it was much busier during rush hour. He stared out the window at the pre-dawn desert-scape, feeling the loneliness of the scene. It was something with which he could identify.

It was a woman who had brought him here. What else could bring a man like him to a dying desert town like this? It was Abigail's hometown. Falling in love with Abby meant falling in love with Geddon. It was an all or nothing situation. And when he married her, he married into the extended family of Geddon.

So many years later, when she died, he buried her in the Geddon Cemetery. Soon after, he considered selling his place and moving away, but quickly dismissed the idea. Even in death, he couldn't bear to leave her behind in thataveyard. Who would buy an old fixer-upper in a town like this anyway?

Something yanked him from his thoughts and memories. He peered into the gray light. Two lights appeared on the road—headlights. A vehicle was approaching the outskirts of town. Recollections pushed to the front of his mind as the vehicle flew along towards the now brightening eastern horizon. It drove toward the dawn; away from the darkness. The similarities between this reality and his all-to-familiar dream was uncanny.

He watched the headlights as they drew nearer his property. He grabbed the flashlight he used for scaring coyotes off his property. He flashed it out his window as the vehicle flashed past, toward the heart of town. The light revealed a dark colored SUV.

He turned off the flashlight and ran to his bedroom. He multi-tasked, removing his pajamas as he went. Time was of the essence.

*

Adam thought he saw a light flash from one of the dark houses as they drove by. He stared at the house he thought it had come from, but everything was dark. The light, if it had been there at all, vanished as quickly as it had appeared. Still, it made Adam wonder.

He drove into the heart of what the homemade sign indicated was Geddon, California. An indicator light glowed on the dash—low fuel. He looked at the fuel gauge. The needle sat on *E.* He was grateful they'd made it to a town. Running out of gas in the desert wouldn't have been a good thing.

He pulled into what must be the town's only filling station. The place was generic. No big names like *Shell* or *Exxon* could be found here. Instead, there was a simple sign: *Geddon Gas and Grocery.* Adam maneuvered the Rogue alongside the sole pump. He frowned. All lights were off. The station was dark, as was the pump. A piece of masking tape held a handwritten sign to the pump. The station, it told him, did not open for three more hours, but fuel could be purchased at any time with a credit or debit card. Adam's frown deepened as he stared at the card reader retrofitted to the pump. He couldn't use plastic and risk giving away their location.

"So what now?" he asked Garrett.

The pastor shrugged. "I guess we're stuck here until it opens."

Adam nodded. He didn't like staying in one place too long, even a place as out in the boonies as Geddon, California. They had no idea where they were going once they got out of this town. They didn't know where they were going period.

The Nissan had a built-in GPS system, but they had refused to use it, unsure if one could be tracked through GPS. Adam wanted to keep moving. He felt safe in movement. He looked at his wife and child. They both slept.

"Crap," came Garrett's voice.

Garrett was looking into the Nissan's side-view mirror. His expression disturbed Adam.

"Someone's seen us," Garrett expounded.

Adam adjusted the rear view to look behind. Garrett was right. They had been noticed. They were being watched.

CHAPTER 31

The expedition made it back to the city in one piece, but this was little comfort to Hunter. The city, great as it was, offered them little protection. The enemy they had encountered in the desert was too powerful.

He was at a loss as to what his next move should be. Their goal had not changed. The egg had to be destroyed. How to get past the demon army that guarded it was the question. Something had to be done. If the egg was allowed to hatch, the beast's time of harvesting souls would begin. And that would be very bad. The city was in peril. If the beast hatched, it would come for them with one goal: their destruction.

If only he knew how much time would pass before the egg cracked. The beast hatched every hundred years, but that knowledge did him little good. It was a hundred years Inner Earth time, but time between the Earths was like two rivers, each flowing independently of the other. A year might be a day on the other side of the Space Between, or vice versa.

It had been twenty years since Nora, himself, and their unborn child had arrived here. He wondered how long it had been on the other side. It had to be less than a hundred years because the egg had not hatched. He had no idea how much time he still had. The last grain of sand could fall through the hourglass at any moment. Such thoughts stressed him.

Over the years, he had thought a lot about those he had cared about in his native Earth; friends, family and others. He wondered if they were still alive, or if they were long dead and cold in their graves. He wondered if any of them wondered about him. It must have been odd how Nora and he had suddenly disappeared.

He stared out into the desert from the edge of the great city. He feared the beast was about to hatch. Fright crept into him and made itself comfortable in the very marrow of his bones.

CHAPTER 32

The occupants of the SUV had seen him. It was hardly surprising, as Matthew made no attempt to hide, but stood behind the vehicle in plain view. Although the sun had not yet crested the horizon, its bright rays penetrated the eastern sky. Still, the light was not sufficient to see those in the car. He could see the driver and passenger both watched him. The reflection of their eyes in the vehicle's mirrors gave them away.

He stood, feeling exposed and unsure of his next move. Abby had always said one of the things she loved about him was his spontaneity. At the moment, he saw it as only a detriment.

The air was cool. Mornings in the desert usually were. This morning felt exceptionally so, but he thought it was because he was covered with nervous perspiration. Of course he would be nervous. It wasn't every day one met up with the physical manifestation of a recurring nightmare.

He tried to deny this was what it was, but his denial fell flat. Dreams didn't, to his knowledge, cross into reality. Yet before him stood the car from his dream. He couldn't see who or what was in the back seat, but he would wager a woman and child occupied that space. He had no doubt the infant would have dark eyes. He shivered as that thought sank in and his icy sweat began to roll down his spine in slow-moving tendrils.

He glanced behind him, but no wall of darkness was seen. Grateful, he turned his attention back to the SUV. His nerves spiked. The driver and passenger doors had opened. Matthew had not planned his next move; now it appeared it was being made for him. He wanted to run away like a child caught eavesdropping. Instead, he planted his feet and stood his ground. He didn't know what to expect. He had to be ready for anything.

CHAPTER 33

Alice was dreaming and she knew it as she slept in the back of the vehicle. This was highly unusual for her. Normally, she was not aware she was dreaming until after she awoke, but this time was different.

She had only ever experienced such strangeness in dreams once before. That time, her dreams were visions of nightmares involving Lucifer and his plot to kill Kerry. That dream had proven true. The Devil had indeed been after Kerry as well as herself. Now, as she dreamt again, she felt the Devil's schemes were far from over.

She didn't understand why Satan wanted her child—not that the 'why' mattered much when Satan targeted you. Hunting season had opened and they were the prey. Her only goal at that moment was to get the Devil off their trail. So far, she felt she was failing.

Her dream was short and repetitive, one skit playing over and over again like a stage rehearsal for the big show to come. In her dream, she stood in a vacant parking lot. It was dark, but she could tell dawn was just around the corner. She held Kerry in her arms; held her close. Fright built to near-panic levels; she felt danger lurking just out of sight, preparing to steal her child. She turned slowly, trying to spot the danger. Her senses tingled.

She tried to see in all directions at once, but she was only one person with one set of eyes. Still, she tried. Details emerged. She stood beside a single gasoline pump in front of a dilapidated filling station. She studied the building, hoping she could find protection there. The lights were out. It appeared to be closed and she knew she would find the doors locked. She would find no hope there.

Something moved. She turned. Something fluttered in a light breeze. On the pump was taped a simple handwritten sign verifying that the station would not open for three hours. *Three hours,* she thought; tears began to track down her cheeks. Her child would surely be stolen and dead long before 180 minutes ticked by.

She turned from the pumps with a jolt. Something had aroused her instincts. Whatever it was, was just out of sight, but coming nearer. Then she saw him. She didn't know where he had come from or how he had managed to get so close so quickly without her noticing.

Regardless, he was there, and very near. She had never seen him before, yet instead of the rising panic she would have expected, the sight of this newcomer de-escalated her nerves. A sense of peace filled her.

She guessed his age to be around sixty. He had a full head of hair, more grey than not, that bushed out uncombed as if he had just gotten out of bed. His skin was dark and leathery as would be expected from a rural man who spent his days out in an arid environment.

She looked him in the eyes. They showed a man of intense gentleness and kindness. "Who are you?" she asked.

He smiled. The smile was pleasant, but it held sadness and loss.

"Who are you?" she asked again. His delay in response did not frighten her, but it did pique her curiosity.

"I am the First Gospel," he answered her.

She had the inkling this was not his God-given name, but a riddle. She thought about it, but the riddle's answer eluded her grasp. "The First Gospel?" she repeated.

He nodded.

"What do you want?"

"I want you and your child to be safe." His voice was as kind as his eyes. Sorrow seemed to run just below the surface, hiding behind the kindness of his voice and using it as a veil.

"We can't be safe," she answered him. "The Devil is after us."

"There are those stronger than the Devil," he assured her. She was about to say more, but he continued. "Stick with me. Live where I live. Stay where I stay. You'll be safe."

*

She woke up and rubbed sleep from her eyes, the dream as crystal-clear as any reality. She looked at Kerry, sleeping beside her in the back seat of the Nissan. She looked to the front seat. Both doors were open and the seats empty. Panic reared. Where were Garrett and Adam?

She expanded her search and spotted them. They were not far, standing outside the vehicle, one on each side, just beyond the doors. Her red flags did not come down, but at least they dropped to half-mast.

Then she saw where they were parked. Her heart skipped a beat as she noticed the single pump with the note fluttering in the breeze. She couldn't read the note. She didn't need to, to know what it said.

In awe, she looked at the darkened station building. A sign identified it as *Geddon Gas and Grocery. Geddon,* she thought. The name meant nothing to her, yet she was sure it was significant.

"Good morning."

She turned around and looked out the back window. She was positive she had never been to Geddon, yet the voice was familiar.

"My name is Matthew," the voice said.

Matthew? The book of Matthew. The first gospel of the New Testament. *The first gospel!*

She tried to get a good look at him, but the first rays of morning sun had broken past the horizon, throwing a glare on the rear window she was trying to see out of. It didn't matter. She knew what he looked like. She had just met him in her dream. Now however, he was meeting her outside the land of dreams. She wondered what it meant. She wondered and quivered.

*

Good morning, he had said. *My name is Matthew,* he had uttered.

Why in the world did he start out that way? It came across cheesy, as if he were some door-to-door vacuum salesman extending his hand to offer a hearty handshake and a good deal on the latest in carpet cleaning technology.

The two men who stood outside the SUV looked at him. They did not look malicious and for that he was thankful. Of course they had no reason for maliciousness. But they outnumbered him, they were younger, and their manner suggested they wanted to be left alone.

At least they came to the right town for that, Matthew thought. But he wondered why. His curiosity was piqued. So were his suspicions. He was right to be cautious, he reminded himself.

The one on the passenger side smiled and nodded acknowledgment of his greeting. The driver did an awkward wave as well. Neither said a word.

They were hiding something. Matthew's nerves danced. Geddon had no law enforcement. They had never needed it and couldn't afford to pay one anyway. Geddonites had always gotten along more or less. But if organized crime syndicates moved in, things could quickly deteriorate.

He didn't think these people were big-time criminals, but he was no expert. And even if they weren't big time, maybe those who were after them were. The citizens of Geddon didn't need that kind of heat.

Unsure what to do, but feeling he needed to do something, Matthew took a small step towards them. That's when he saw the woman sitting in the back seat, her face almost glued to the rear window. She had a strange look on her face and he felt she knew about his dream. His heart began to race. He tried to smile and brush down his crazy hair which he had not taken the time to comb down. He forced a grin and was sure it looked more creepy than friendly. *Great.* He was not sure what to do next. His lack of a plan was painfully evident.

The one standing on the driver's side broke the silence. "You work here?"

Matthew shook his head. He wanted to say more, but nothing came out. He wasn't sure what words would make this little rendezvous less awkward so he remained silent, which didn't help.

"Do you know if there's a way to get gas here in this town at this time of the morning?" one of the men asked.

"Do you have a credit or debit card?" Matthew pointed to the card reader on the pump.

The two men glanced at each other. "No, we don't," the one on the driver's side mumbled.

Matthew was finally finding his voice. "Well, this is the only filling station in town and there ain't no other town around here for miles."

The two men glanced at each other across the roof of their vehicle. Their expressions confirmed for Matthew what he had suspected. They were hiding something.

"You folks just passing through?" he asked, trying for the friendly small town feel.

Both men paused and then nodded and Matthew knew they were lying. Nobody ever 'passed through' Geddon. The road leading into town came from nowhere and led to nowhere. He tried to put them at some level of ease, hoping to learn more. "There's nothing that can be done about your gas situation for a few hours, but if you guys are hungry, I'd be happy to host breakfast at my house. It's not far from here."

He could barely believe what he was saying. He was not the type to invite strangers into his home, especially suspicious strangers. Then again, he had never met the likes of these—dream-characters existing in reality.

As leery as he was of inviting them into his home, he expected they would be just as cautious being invited. For all they knew, he could be a sociopath killer who lured those who were 'just passing through' into his home to murder them and fashion their skin into clothing to be worn at the annual Sociopath Killer Ball. Of course he was nothing of the sort, but they didn't know that.

The men reacted as he'd expected, with nervous apprehension. He was sure they were about to decline on his offer, when the woman from the back seat rolled down her window. "What did he say?" she asked.

"He invited us to breakfast," the leery answer came from the one who had his arm in a sling.

"We would love to do breakfast with you," she said without hesitation.

The men didn't look happy with her acceptance at all.

Matthew pretended not to notice the chill on their faces. "Great."

The thought suddenly occurred to him that he may not have enough food in the home to carry through on his promise. He was just an old widower after all and didn't keep copious amounts of provisions in stash, but it was too late now to retract the offer. It was much too late.

*

We would love to do breakfast with you? Alice cringed inwardly. What had possessed her to say such a thing? Deep down, she knew the answer. This was the man from her vision. From her past experience, things like that should not be ignored or forgotten.

She glanced at Garrett and Adam. They were a tad more skeptical than she was. Could she blame them? The answer was clear: no–not really. This man was a complete stranger. He was less so to her, but how were they to know she had just met Matthew, the First Gospel? There was value in this 'chance' meeting. She just had to learn what that value was. Given their situation, it could be something worth more than gold. It could be something that might save their very lives.

She got out of the Nissan and stretched muscles grown stiff from sleeping in the back seat. A good breakfast would do her some good.

"I'm Alice." She extended her hand towards him.

He took her hand and shook it. She had learned over the years that you could discover a surprising amount of information about somebody by the way they shook hands. Matthew's was firm—a good sign.

"Glad to meet you, Alice." His voice was friendly, if a little uncertain.

Of course he would be uncertain. Unlike her, who had the privilege of already having met him, she was nothing but a stranger from his perspective.

"So, breakfast?" he said more questioningly than matter of fact.

"Breakfast would be wonderful," Alice confirmed. She avoided looking at Garrett or Adam. She imagined their expressions were less-than-approving.

"Well then, I'll lead the way. My home isn't far from here."

"Sure," Alice answered. "Hop in."

Matthew got in the back seat as if it was the most normal thing in the world to hop into a car full of strangers.

She used this opportunity to communicate with Adam and Garrett. "Trust me," she whispered. "This guy is legit."

Adam and Garrett exchanged glances. Their expressions was not a vote of confidence.

She got in the back seat opposite the newcomer. Kerry slept between them. He stared at Kerry—an odd stare, his mouth slightly open, his eyes wide.

When he noticed that she was watching him, he looked away. "Can I ask you a question?" he said after a moment.

"Sure." Her voice did not sound sure at all.

"What color are your child's eyes?"

What kind of a question was that? Something was up. This First Gospel character knew more than he was leading on. Why else would he bring up Kerry's eyes; those deep brown, unusual eyes.

She looked down at the sleeping baby. "Why do you ask?"

CHAPTER 34

"Here is wisdom. Let he that hath understanding count the number of the beast: for it is the number of man; and his number is six hundred threescore and six." – Revelation 13:18.

*

JoAnne was busier than a one-legged woman in a butt-kicking contest and had been ever since her job had been given to her. She washed down stimulants with energy drinks to keep going. She had to keep going.

Her lot in life had been reduced to the monotonous routine of tattooing the same tattoo over and over and over again. The only break to that monotony was the fact that she shifted from tattooing foreheads to right palms and back again. Of course this shift back and forth was a pattern in and of itself and created its own monotony within the monotony and was therefore little consolation.

She had been doing it for only a few days, being given only enough breaks to get short naps, empty her bladder and bowels, and massage the cramps out of her hands. She looked at the growing pile of dice on the table next to her. Every Seeker laid their set of three dice on that table in exchange for their tattoos. They'd been told they no longer needed the dice. The tattoos were the symbol of the new order and all that was needed.

She looked at her own tattoo which she had done herself. The palm had been easy enough. Her forehead had been more of a challenge, the mirror throwing her left/right orientation off. Still, she had accomplished the task. If she was honest with herself, she wasn't sure she wanted to be a member of this new order. But she dared not question her new masters. She suspected such questions did not bode well with these newcomers.

She looked down on the palm of her current client. She needed to focus, but lack of sleep and the monotony of her new life made it difficult. She had to focus on the three-digit image she had been assigned to emblazon on all who came to her.

666: the symbol of the new order. There was no more need for dice. There was no more need to ask how high one could roll. There would be no more need to respond with the proper response. 666 was all that was needed.

Seeker after Seeker came, rejected their dice and received the mark. She was so exhausted. Yet, she continued as she suspected she must. When she had started the work, she had one consolation—once the Ra's ink ran dry, she would have to stop. Now, she felt like crying. The ink did not run dry. It was like magic.

Her body screamed, telling her to quit. She needed a break. She stared at the line that had formed. No break would be given. She continued. If only she could take a break without being caught. She considered it, but she feared the consequences. She continued.

Of course she might *not* get caught, but she had not grown weary enough yet to put her new masters to that test. Perhaps, she would soon be desperate enough to risk it, but not now. For now, she continued.

She knew what she was: a slave to the Ra. As a slave, her only value was in doing as she was ordered until she was told to stop. She had not been told to stop. She sank deeper into her despair, but she kept working.

CHAPTER 35

Matthew had climbed into the back seat of the Rogue with reservations. Dream or no dream, getting into a car with strangers went against every fiber of common sense. He studied the baby who slept beside him. Her eyes remained closed. Alice had not answered his question regarding the color of those eyes. It didn't matter. He knew.

He directed the driver to his house, hoping he had something, anything to feed them. He tried to think, but couldn't remember if he'd stocked his pantry lately.

Their silence was unnerving. Their demeanor reminded him he was in the presence of those trying to escape from something. His vision hinted they were running from something dark. He felt he'd been tasked with protecting them from that something, but in order to do that, he would need answers. *Perhaps over breakfast,* he thought. *Perhaps over breakfast.*

The drive to his house would take mere minutes which was the time needed to go about anywhere in Geddon. Regardless, Matthew felt uneasy. He wanted to get there as quickly as possible.

As they drove, he turned and peered out the rear window, half-expecting to see the consuming darkness on their tail. He saw nothing however, just Geddon Gas and Grocery as they drove away from it. Still, he felt that somewhere, an evil something was searching for a dark-colored Nissan Rogue. He didn't want to be in that vehicle when it was found. *Drive faster!*

These were odd times. Even in his backwater burg Matthew had heard what was going down outside of his little California haven. The Ra had arrived. He wondered if this little rag-tag group was running from these newcomers to Earth. He couldn't blame them. There was something about the Ra that rubbed him wrong. He couldn't put his finger on it—just a quality that made his skin crawl.

He forced himself to turn forward in his seat. As at most crossroads, it would do no good to keep looking back.

When they reached his house, he asked if they would mind parking the Nissan in the empty bay of his two car garage. They didn't mind. In fact, they seemed relieved. Clearly they preferred to have their car out of sight. They parked. The garage door came down behind. They exited the Nissan. Together, they entered Matthew's home.

CHAPTER 36

Lucifer waited for Bob to arrive. He waited and frowned. He was not used to waiting. His power had been untethered. His reign on Earth had begun, yet things were progressing far too slowly. Patience was a virtue he had never possessed and no amount of power, untethered or otherwise, could change that. He paced the room. *Where in damnation was Bob?*

He took a deep breath. He rubbed his temples with the slender tips of his index fingers and tried to calm his mind, but his mind refused calming. The thoughts of all that needed to be done haunted him. He had to give out his mark upon all of mankind. All who refused...? He would give them an offer no one in their right mind would dare turn down.

His scowl deepened. The governments of the world were stepping aside for him. Presidents and Kings were now vassals under his reign. More and more were receiving his mark. Regardless, one thing gnawed at him.

Despite his untethered power, he still needed to eliminate the infant Gatekeeper. He'd tried once, and almost succeeded. This time, he would not fail. He tried to use his new power to locate the child, but apparently untethered power was not the same as unlimited power. His frown deepened further. He closed his eyes, trying harder, but nothing came to him.

He heard a noise and opened his eyes. Before him, stood Bob. His frown turned upside-down. He liked Bob. What was there not to like? The answer was *nothing*. Here was a true believer of lies and one who would remain loyal even to death. "What took you so long?" he asked.

Bob did not answer. Instead, he looked down, a sign of submission.

Lucifer breathed in deeply and caught the scent of fear wafting from this slave of his. He loved that scent. It was good Bob feared him. Fear was one of the great tools of manipulation. He inhaled again and immersed himself in the buzz the scent created in him. "I asked you a question. I expect an answer." He watched Bob quiver. "What took you so long?"

"I was getting the report you wanted, from JoAnne." Bob's voice was as submissive as his appearance.

"And why did that take so long?"

"You must forgive JoAnne, but she is exhausted. Her report was barely comprehensible. She needs a break."

If Bob had been anyone else, Lucifer would have killed him then and there and consumed his soul like a dollop of caviar on a cracker, savoring every last ounce. *How dare this mortal tell him to show forgiveness!* Forgiveness was a weakness of the enemy, something he was not capable of. Yes, it was lucky for Bob he had such great value to his master at the moment. That value was a saving grace—for now. "Where is JoAnne?" he asked.

"She is where you left her, doing her task."

"Lead me to her."

Bob nodded. He looked as if he were about to cry.

He led Lucifer out of the room. Lucifer allowed Bob to lead him, at least for the time being.

CHAPTER 37

Mathew stared at the four visitors. The three adults took up three of the four chairs at his dining room table. The baby rested in her car seat upon the floor. He had not had so many guests in his home since his wife's funeral and felt a little out of sorts.

He watched them from his kitchen, under the ruse of getting breakfast ready. In reality he wasn't moving very quickly to that end. He was more preoccupied watching them interact with one another. The only one of the four who looked relaxed was the infant. The others were all fidgety. *Why?* he wondered. He hoped to gain answers over breakfast.

To his dismay, the only food he found in sufficient supply that would pass for anything resembling breakfast was a box of off-brand shredded wheat which he'd bought more for regularity than anything else. Despite this lack of provisions, he couldn't help but smile. His late wife had always told him his miserly ways would come to haunt him and now, here he was entertaining guests with generic fiber. He hoped he at least had milk.

He opened his fridge, holding his breath with anticipation. There he saw a half-gallon of skim milk. He exhaled with relief. He eyed the expiration date and frowned. That date had come and gone two days ago. He removed the jug's cap and sniffed. It smelled okay. He didn't own a dairy cow and Geddon Gas and Grocery was still closed, so it would have to do.

He loaded up a stack of bowls, spoons, and napkins and added them to a tray with the box of cereal and the borderline milk. He entered the dining room carrying it all and holding his breath. They were still there. They had not bolted. Again, he exhaled.

For the first time, he saw the child's eyes. The baby was awake and feeding on a bottle of formula. Her eyes were dark brown, almost black. It came as no surprise. In fact, it was expected. "So," he said as he distributed the items from the tray. "What brings you to this little neck of the woods?"

None of them responded and Matthew wondered if he was coming across too hokey for their comparatively urban likes. In reality, he had no idea if they were urban or not, but chances were, at the very least they were from a bigger place than Geddon. Plus, he had noticed in their car, the ignition system used a screwdriver in lieu of keys. Car thieves were more common in urban areas.

"We're just passing through," the woman finally answered.

Matthew looked at her. He had a feeling about her in particular. She knew more than she was letting on. He needed to learn what she knew. He racked his brain, but couldn't think of a good way to ask more, not without raising their suspicions further. With a sigh, Matthew spoke. "I am going to level with you. I have been having these…"

"Before you go any further," the woman interrupted. "I need to let you know something. I had a vision about you."

He stopped mid-sentence and took a moment to close his gaping mouth. He had been about to divulge his dreams.

"I've had visions like this before about other things and they've always proven true. We need you to protect us."

Matthew opened his mouth, but no words came. He'd been worried about shocking them and now they threw this curve ball. *Wow*, he thought. *How the tables have turned.*

CHAPTER 38

En route to check on JoAnne, Lucifer sequestered Splinter. Thus far, he had been pleased with this demon's performance, a true master of lies. Now he needed him for another task. "Walk with me," Lucifer said. Splinter fell into line beside his master.

Bob led the way, past the line of people waiting for their tattoos, to the room where JoAnne worked. JoAnne stood with her tattoo gun in hand, but there was no one in the tattoo chair. She was not doing her job.

Lucifer glared at her, hoping to push her back to her task with fear, but she didn't even flinch. She simply stood there still as stone with the exception of an occasional twitch.

"See," Bob indicated the twitchy woman before them. "I told you she needs a rest."

Abruptly, JoAnne's eyes widened as if she had just noticed them. "Stay back!" she shrieked.

This command irked Lucifer. *How dare this mortal command me!* His first thought was to punish her. But she still had value to him that would diminish if he punished now.

He forced a smile and caught the scent of mental illness in the air—a scent he loved almost as much as fear. It wafted from her in clouds. It was delicious and his smile became less forced.

"Stay back," she said again. "There are bugs everywhere. They'll bite you if you get too close. They're mighty bitey bugs."

Bob chimed in. "You see. I don't know if you Ra need to sleep, but we humans do. This is what happens when we don't."

"Give her more energy drinks," Splinter chimed in.

"No!" JoAnne shrieked. "No more energy drinks. That's where the bugs came from, the mighty bitey bugs."

Lucifer breathed in all the insanity-laced air his immortal body could hold. He held it deep inside before exhaling it out like the smoke inhaled from a fine cigar. Sadly, there was no time to relish this rush. They needed everyone to get the mark. There was no time for rest.

"Splinter," he said.

"Yes, Lord," Splinter responded.

"You know what must be done."

Splinter nodded as a grin grew on his face.

Lucifer escorted Bob from the room. Splinter and JoAnne needed privacy. Besides, he had another task for Bob. He closed the door and left Splinter with JoAnne.

"I'm sorry, folks, there will be a slight delay in you getting your new tattoos. Do be patient. The artist needs a break."

CHAPTER 39

Garrett stared blankly at Alice. Then he shifted his eyes to their host. He looked the man over. Matthew was no Arnold Swartzeneger or Sylvester Stalone. He did not appear to be the type who was able to protect them. Especially given that they needed protection from all the powers of Hell.

He guessed Matthew was between 55 and 60 give or take. He was slightly slumped and showing the wear of living in the arid land. He looked back to Alice. If she thought this guy could protect them, who was he to argue? She had never been wrong with her visions before. Still, his faith teetered. He frowned. Given what he had already been through, he should have faith as strong as granite. God had protected them before from foes unimaginable, in quite unexpected ways. So, why now couldn't this man hide them from evils no worse than before? *God, help me with my unbelief.*

Garret looked at Adam. Adam was focused on Matthew, a stoic expression on his face. He wondered if Adam was also struggling to understand God's mysterious ways.

Finally, he looked down at Kerry. His source of deepest questions lay with her. He wondered why the Devil wanted this child so badly, this innocent child. Weren't there countless other souls on earth more deserving of demonic torture? Regardless of these issues of faith, he decided, he understood enough. He needed to keep this child hidden from the enemy. If God had chosen this new acquaintance to help in that mission, so be it.

He looked once again at Matthew. He would need to focus on a journey of faith-building and that journey would start here and now.

CHAPTER 40

"And there came out of the smoke locusts upon the earth and unto them was given power as the scorpions of the earth have power. And it was commanded them that they should not hurt the grass of the earth, neither any green thing, neither any tree, but only those men which have not the seal of God in their foreheads." – Revelation 9:3-4.

*

JoAnne was not in her right mind but was right enough to realize it. She knew the mighty bitey bugs were not normal, and she suspected they weren't even real. She couldn't recall ever seeing such swarms before.

They were thick as locusts, yet they weren't locusts. They were powerful like warhorses. On their heads, they wore what looked like crowns, but may have been crests. They had sharp teeth. Usually long hair covered their faces, but on occasion a glimpse showed them to be almost human, fiendishly human. But it was their tails that disconcerted her more than all the rest. Those tails, with their shiny black tips and venomous moisture reminded her of scorpions.

There were other things in the room as well. In her current state of mind, these other things seemed grotesque. On the table was the pile of dice. She didn't like the way the dots on the dice stared at her like beady little eyes. The bugs terrorized her while the dice watched. The bugs drew nearer, eyes stared harder. She felt ill.

"This is all an illusion," she said to herself. She wanted it to be an illusion. Still, the bugs and the dice seemed so real. She suddenly realized there was another presence in the room with her. This one was no illusion. She felt him like the chill of an arctic wind. She had seen him before. *Sprinter?* No, that wasn't quite right. *Sliver?*

"Call me Splinter," he said as if sensing her thoughts. He drew near and cold solidified in her bones. She began to shiver.

He walked up to her and the mighty bitey bugs parted before him as if paying homage to nobility. The dice no longer watched. They all looked away as if what was about to go down was too disturbing to watch.

Her fear escalated. She wasn't sure what was about to happen, but the bugs and dice were preferable to the entity that approached. She stumbled back. He lunged for her. She turned to escape. In her sleep-deprived state, she collided with the table of dice, lost her balance, and tumbled to the floor. The dice tumbled with her. The bugs scattered from the deluge of falling dice and table.

In the chaos, Splinter drew closer.

Panicking, she scurried back from him along with the mighty bitey bugs. But she was slow and awkward. In a flash, he had her. She thrashed in his grip, desperate to escape. Laughter echoed in her ears. The mighty bitey bugs were laughing at her! The hundreds of dice scattered around her watched with beady little eyes, no longer looking away as if appalled, but staring with interest and lust.

She struggled harder, but Splinter's grip was solid. She couldn't get away. He entered her. The instant he was inside her, everything around her grew calm. The bugs no longer laughed. The dice no longer stared. The outer calm however did not match on the inside. Inside, she squirmed, but no longer to escape. Getting away was impossible.

Now that one possessed her, she saw past their disguise, and what she saw was horrible. The Ra were demons; vile, dirty, and scarred. She wanted to warn the others. She had to warn the others! Her possessor forbade it. She cowered deep within herself, but even in the furthest reaches of her soul, the demon lurked. There was nowhere for her to hide.

She realized then that all of the terror she had ever experienced was child's play compared to the terror that invaded her. She begged for relief. She was ignored.

CHAPTER 41

Matthew sat, dumbfounded, between Alice, Adam, and Garrett. The story was beyond his ability to believe. And yet, it made sense. Television shows no longer played and music was gone from all radio frequencies. Now, only news dominated the airwaves, and it was always the same. Only stories pertaining to the "arrival of the benevolent alien species" were heard on any medium and that included the internet.

Even before these newcomers told their story, he had suspected the Ra were not who they claimed to be. Although no representatives of the Ra had arrived in Geddon, the media had been advertising a 'new life' for all who came to the Ra to receive their mark of loyalty.

The story he heard from the ones who sat at his breakfast table answered many of his questions. However, it also opened new ones. Why was Lucifer after such a defenseless child? What secret did this baby hold that angered and frustrated the demons so much? To what length would the demons go through to extract said secret, and what would happen to anyone harboring such a fugitive?

The answers to his 'whys' didn't matter. That the Devil was after her was enough. He became convinced more than ever that he must protect this child at all costs, keep her safe and hidden. He looked at the group set on protecting this child with him and fought in himself to ward off self-condemning feelings, to push away questions that made him sick. *What were they against? All the powers of Hell? How could he think they had a chance to win such a fight?*

Their only hope rested with God. Only through Him, could they fly below the enemy's radar; out of sight. Despite the dire situation, he smiled. He knew now why he had been chosen to be their protector. It was not because he was strong, or intelligent, or conniving. No, in this case, it was, as in real estate: location—location—location. Geddon California was nearly non-existent. It did not appear on GPS or on any maps. It was known only to those who lived there and those who happened to stumble upon it.

He hoped location would be enough. It was his only hope. It was his prayer.

CHAPTER 42

The mighty bitey bugs had left; the staring dice stared no more. Her fatigue evaporated. Despite these positives, JoAnne found no relief. Where before, she had trouble remembering his name, now it stood out crystal-clear. His name was Splinter. This demon possession sullied and violated her. He forced her to rise from the floor. She didn't want to rise, but she had little choice. Her new master commanded it.

She rose. He forced her to pick up her tattoo tools, which she did. He called in the next client to receive the mark. He called, but it was her voice. He forced her to resume her work and she did. He spoke inside her as she tattooed the next in line. "Do you know how many are waiting to be given the mark of the Ra?"

The mark of the Ra? She knew now no such mark existed. It was the mark of Satan she was administering; the mark of eternal damnation. Within her tortured soul, she heard Splinter laugh, a cruel laugh. She would receive no sympathy, only ridicule, from the one that shared her body. She stared down at the work she was now doing. It was her hands guiding the art. It was her knowledge directing the needle. Yet it was not her.

She looked at the new tattoo, glistening with wet ink and blood—666. The sight of those numbers made her sick. Again, Splinter taunted her with his laughter. She wanted desperately to get away, but there was nowhere, even within herself, to run. He was everywhere, mocking and taunting without mercy.

Thoughts of her future scared her. She had the feeling this unholy marriage was permanent and binding. *And the two shall become one flesh.* Although God had not joined them, she felt sure man could not separate.

"Please let me go," she begged inside herself. "I promise I won't tell anyone if you just let me go."

Splinter laughed a cold laugh. "I'm no fool, JoAnne." His voice echoed in her mind. "You know who we are. You know too much. No, I cannot let you leave. Not ever! You are mine!"

One client left and another entered. The tattooing started again, a perpetual cycle. Now, under the influence of immortal demons, she saw her work progress at obscene speeds. She could never have done such flawless work so quickly on her own. It struck her she was nothing more than a tool of the Devil, a machine for their unholy purposes. She shuddered as she wondered what would happen if she, the machine, broke or ceased to be of use. Or what would happen when no more tattoos were required. She shuddered and a frightened cry escaped her.

"Don't worry." She heard his voice in her mind. "You'll be useful for a very long time, JoAnne. Just think of how many there are on this planet who will want these marks." Splinter laughed again. "It looks like you have quite a backlog."

A client left. Another entered. JoAnne felt like vomiting.

*

Splinter was in ecstasy, utter ecstasy. He loved the act of possession. It was his birthright. More than usual, he loved to possess JoAnne. She was so weak, a ball of clay waiting to be molded by demonic arts. He loved being the master sculptor. He breathed in and tasted her terror on his tongue. It tasted wonderful. He licked her soul and felt it squirm as he shuddered with pleasure.

She tried to retreat from him and the chase was on. The hunter pursued the hunted. The prey ran from the predator. He played the game for a moment; teasing her, taunting her. There was nowhere for her to run. But he grew tired of the game. He took her and stroked her harshly. She was his possession, his tool. He had plans for this tool, big plans. He would use her until she was worn down to nothing. When the ride was done, he would throw her aside.

He tested his tool. It was sturdy, only a few miles on the odometer. He had much to do with her and many miles to tack on. He laughed out loud through her vocal chords so that his tool could hear. He felt her shrink away as he laughed and that was good. A good tool fears the master.

He inhaled her terror; what a wonderful scent. It would be a pleasure to complete this time of possession. It would be especially satisfying to hear the tool finally crack under the pressure.

CHAPTER 43

A few days had passed since they'd stumbled upon Geddon. Alice chuckled. The plan had been to fill the Rogue's gas tank and move on. Moving on had been their strategy all along; perpetual motion—it was harder to draw a bead on a moving target. The hope was, it would confuse the enemy and improve their chances of survival.

Amending this plan had not come easily as a single mistake could prove fatal. But after a group meeting, and a prayer led by Pastor Garrett, they agreed to stay for the time being under the watchful eye of Matthew.

Already she saw that staying put was not a bad decision. In the short time since the demons had arrived, they had overwhelmed much of the planet with their influence and had spies almost everywhere. If reports could be believed, very few places were free of them. Geddon was free— for now. She hoped it would stay that way. Meeting Matthew had been a Godsend. Because of him, they had become secret citizens of the hidden berg of Geddon California.

Alice wondered if this forgotten village could keep them safe forever. She doubted it, and worried what would happen when their location was discovered. She shook the worries off. It did no good to dwell on them. For the time being, they would live with Matthew. For the time being, they were safe. For the time being, they were alive.

PART TWO

Seeker's Salvation Day + 50 years

CHAPTER 44

Bob Gulam was doing his job—a job he'd been doing for five decades now. Despite his long hours, he had not grown weary. This was his passion, his love. In fifty years, he hadn't aged a day. The Ra had rewarded him well for his faith in them. They had given him, it seemed, the gift of immortality.

Of all the Union of the Ra members, he only knew of one other who had received this elixir of life—JoAnne. Of the two of them however, he had fared far better. JoAnne, though still young-looking, had a beaten-down, haggard look. She had a vacant stare in her eyes, as if on death row with all pardons exhausted.

Bob often wondered why he looked so invigorated while she looked so spent. He could only speculate, but thought it might have to do with the fact that while he was doing what he loved, she was not. Maybe tattooing 666 on hands and foreheads, over and over and over again was not her passion. Also, she did not sleep. He had asked her about it once. She told him she no longer required sleep. By the look of her, he guessed she was wrong.

As for Bob, he slept when needed, but when he wasn't sleeping he was working for his boss Lucifer. His job was his mission. He was the town crier, tasked with convincing the inhabitants of Earth to receive the mark and be joined to the Union.

Why would anyone refuse such a gift? As crazy as it seemed, some did. He firmly believed these people were fundamentally flawed. There was no other explanation. The Ra, in their infinite kindness, had given clear orders regarding those who refused the gift. He was to be patient with those flawed humans. He was to continue to attempt to persuade them.

Bob sometimes felt he didn't have the patience to deal with those who refused to join the way of truth. When he slept, he often dreamed of the genocide he wished he could inflict upon these stupid people. Personally, he wanted the planet rid of them, but orders were orders. He obeyed.

The staunchest opponents were generally of the Christian persuasion. He hated Christians. Of all people, they were the most closed-minded, refusing the mercy of the Ra at every opportunity. They called him the Antichrist for Pete's sake. On some level, they were right. He opposed Christ.

Why shouldn't he? Jesus Christ was a sham, a pipe dream. Jesus' absence was Bob's proof. Where was this savior now? Where was this King of Kings and Lord of Lords? He was nowhere to be seen—because he didn't exist. What did exist was Lucifer and the Ra. They were the true saviors, the true messiahs. The sooner all humans accepted the truth, the better. He longed for the time when all were in agreement on this point. Then and only then could the Kingdom of the Ra reign supreme and forever.

Oh, he'd heard all the arguments Christians spouted out their ignorant pie holes. *Jesus is not absent,* they said. *The spirit of Jesus lives in our hearts,* they blabbed. He always heard them out in conjunction with his agreement to maintain patience, but it was so hard. Their words were so full of crap it drove him nuts.

Bob had one consolation in all of this. Without saying it outright, Lucifer had hinted he would not tolerate the insolence of Christians forever. As time passed, the pressure Lucifer allowed on the non-marked would grow more compelling. Finally, the few who were so bull-headed as to refuse the mark of the Ra would be eliminated as part of a final solution.

So to Bob, the message of the Ra (or the Antichrist based on one's prospective) was simple. *Join the Ra. Time is a finite commodity. Once it runs out, so does the choice to join.* He eagerly waited for that time to arrive. He longed for that time. He had to be patient, but it was so difficult.

CHAPTER 45

*

"And then no man might buy or sell, save that he had the mark." –
Revelation 13:17

*

Zach was down in the dumps, literally—he and the rest of the refugees living there. He remembered the good old days, days of steady employment and decent paychecks. Those days were long gone. They had evaporated proportionately as the Ra's influence had increased.

From his point of view, non-marked people were treated much as the Jews of 1930s Nazi Germany. At least some of the Jews were able to escape Deutschland before the borders closed. Such was not the case with the non-marked. There was no border to cross, no place to escape *to*. The whole planet was against them. What the Nazis had done in a decade, the Ra had taken five to do. Still, the end result was the same. With the pressure placed upon the non-marked, their numbers were slowly but steadily decreasing, and those who were left felt an ever-tightening pinch. For Zach, caving into the Ra's new theology was not an option. He believed in the Bible; he saw through the treachery.

The enemy was confident in their deception. Their leader didn't even try to hide his true name. *Lucifer,* Zach thought. The name infuriated him. *King of the Ra? No, King of Hell was more applicable.* The Ra had worked hard to discredit truth, spreading the story throughout the world that Lucifer had been *mistaken* by ancient Hebrews and Christians as the Devil and that was why his name was synonymous with the name of Satan today. *What a crock.*

Things had reached a new low for the unmarked. Under the latest decree from the Ra, no one could buy or sell unless they had the mark, and that included necessities—food, shelter, clothing. The unmarked, as a result, had become a destitute bunch. It mattered little for Zach. You couldn't buy anything anyway, if you had no money. You couldn't get money without a job. And because the Ra controlled all employment, he was out of luck and had been for quite some time.

Again, images of 1930s Germany flooded his mind. The similarities were uncanny. What worried him even more was how 1930s Germany had given birth to 1940s Germany, and how 1940s Germany had evolved from discrimination to genocide.

He trembled. Such thoughts frightened him.

CHAPTER 46

Kerry looked out the front window of Matthew's home. She smiled. She still thought of this house as 'Matthew's home,' though Matthew had been dead and gone for over thirty years.

Her smile diminished. She was not sad Matthew was gone. It had been his time to depart and his suffering was over. What made her sad was that everyone she held close had died or was now dying. She heard her mother cry out. Kerry ran to her.

Alice lay on the old thread-bare couch that had been in Matthew's living room for as long as Kerry could remember. She looked down at her aged mother. It would not be long now.

Alice had changed over the years. Her hair was white like snow. Her skin was wrinkled as a prune, her bones no longer supporting the scant meat upon them.

"Kerry," she called out a second time. Her eyes were wide, though Kerry stood right over her. She was never sure if her mother perceived her presence. This second calling was weaker than the first, yet sounded as if it had taken more effort—not a good sign.

"I'm right here, Mother."

Alice smiled faintly, a peaceful smile. Kerry tried to smile back, but faltered. She thought of Garrett's grave out in the Geddon Cemetery, and her father's beside it. There was an open grave beside her father's. She had dug it herself just that morning. Soon the entire ghost town of Geddon minus one would reside in that cemetery. That's what happens when nobody comes and nobody leaves. A place dies out.

Still, Kerry was thankful Geddon had been a forgotten and lost town. The qualities that made it lonely also made it her haven. She knew the story, how her parents had hidden her from the Ra. She needed to know the whole story, they said, because someday, their time would pass, and she would need to know how to survive in a world conquered by demons. She shuddered. Their time of passing had arrived. Soon, it would be only her, the lone warrior.

She felt her own face with her hand. What kind of warrior could she be? she thought as she felt the wrinkles of her own face. She was in her fifties, no spring chick.

Kerry wondered if Lucifer still searched for her after all this time. But she knew. She didn't understand why demons were after her, but they were. She looked down at her last remaining companion, her own mother. A tear trickled down her cheek. This little piece of the California desert was all she had ever known. Her parents had homeschooled her. Uncle Garrett had instructed her in the Christian faith in which she had grown. Much of her education had involved television and radio broadcasts filled with the rhetoric of the Ra, countered by the truth about the propaganda and what the Ra really were. She knew the truth. She believed it with all her heart.

Given the message the Ra sent, she had a hard time believing so much of the world had turned to them. It seemed, if the media could be believed, that everyone was lining up to receive the mark of the Ra. Then again, why wouldn't the world flock to those who granted prosperity if they aligned with them and poverty if they did not? She had been fortunate to be taken into the little forgotten berg. Geddon might well be the last speck of freedom on the entire planet.

Kerry took Alice's hand in her own. It was cold. The skin was so soft it seemed there was nothing holding it to her mother's old bones. Alice tried to speak, but no words came. "It's okay, mom." Kerry tried to sound brave. "I'm here."

Alice stared at her daughter. Kerry wasn't sure if Alice saw her or was simply staring off. She squeezed her hand and her mother responded with a distant smile. "Can I get you something?"

Alice seemed to come back to the present. "I think I was dreaming," she said.

Kerry nodded but said nothing. She was unsure what to say.

"It was a most interesting dream."

"You don't have to tell me now, mom," Kerry said. "Wait until you get better."

Kerry knew her mother was not going to get better, but it seemed so laborious for her to speak. She didn't want to put her through undue stress.

"Now." Alice pushed back. "I have to tell you now."

Kerry resigned to her mother's insistence. "Fine. Tell me."

"The dreams used to be different when I was younger. They used to be bolder, stronger. They used to be more than mere dreams. They used to be visions."

Kerry felt her mother's grip tighten as she spoke. *Relax,* she wanted to tell her, but did not, out of parental respect. Also, her curiosity was piqued. She wanted to hear about the dream that used to be a vision.

"I dreamt of a voice I had not heard since you were little. It was the voice of Love. Back when you were small, this voice spoke to me and Garrett and helped us in our time of trouble."

"What did the voice say today?" Kerry wanted to know.

Alice hesitated. Her mouth moved as if forming the words pained her. "Love explained to me why Lucifer wants you so badly," she finally said with little more than a whisper.

Kerry was now very interested.

"I now know who Love is," Alice whispered. "Or was. She was the last guard of the Hundred-year-old door."

Kerry nodded as if this all made sense. It did not.

"You are the current guard of the hundred-year-old door; the gatekeeper. That is why Lucifer wants you dead. Love passed her gift to you when she died, back when you were being born."

Kerry nodded again, though it still made no sense. She wondered if her mother was in her right mind. She was on her death bed, after all, and sometimes tendrils of dementia crept in during those final hours. She looked into her mother's eyes. They showed fatigue, but they were clear and did not hint at any lack of cognition.

"Kerry, do you remember the door?"

Kerry thought. She wasn't sure if she was thinking of the door her mother was referring to.

Alice stared intently into the dark brown eyes of her daughter and a thin smile crept on her lips. "You know, I can tell."

"The door in the basement? Is that the door you mean?"

Alice nodded weakly.

Kerry knew. It was an old door. It had once been yellow, but it was hard to tell now. Age and damage had stripped most of the paint. It still had a black knob, which had always reminded her of a large, bulbous eye. Matthew had purchased the door years ago in the time B.R. (before Ra). He didn't need a door, but a salvage man had sold it to him cheap as he passed through town. Matthew had always said he'd purchased it for two reasons. First, it was a fine example of a practical item as folk-art. And secondly, the price was right, and Matthew, miser that he was, couldn't walk away from a good deal.

The salvage man had a story to go with the art, which made the door just that much cooler. Matthew had told the story so many times over the years that Kerry could still recite it word for word.

The door, the salvage man had said, was all that had been left of an old antique shop that had mysteriously exploded, killing the owner and throwing antiques for blocks around. For decades, the door had hung on a wall in Matthew's basement—a door to nowhere. Kerry had always been attracted to it. It was more than appreciation of folk-art. She had been known throughout her years to stare at it endlessly.

"That door is the door you are to guard," Alice said with conviction.

"Why am I to guard it?" she asked.

Alice stared blankly. Finally, she shrugged.

Kerry wondered what could possibly come through that door that was worse than what had already arrived. What could be worse than Satan?

"The voice of Love wanted me to warn you the door must be guarded diligently until you are a century old. Then you will be given knowledge."

"Knowledge?" Her mother's statements were so cryptic.

Alice nodded. "You will know what to do when the time is right. You must simply be ready to receive knowledge."

Kerry nodded and wiped a tear from her eyes.

"I love you, my daughter. You know that, don't you?"

"Of course, Mamma." She had not referred to her mother as 'Mamma' since she was a child. Yet now, it felt right.

Alice exhaled. She did not inhale again. Her hand grew limp in her daughter's hand and fell free. As the soul departed, Kerry draped a sheet over her mother's body. Then she cried.

CHAPTER 47

Zach woke with a start. Had he been dreaming? No, it was more than a dream. It had to be. He had seen a woman with very dark brown eyes. Soft brown hair hung in a long braid down her back, with gray showing at the temples. She was not young. Nor was she old, but middle-aged. She was in a room, all alone, her loneliness palpable, radiating out from her as heat from a stoked furnace. He felt drawn to her, even now that the vision had ceased.

He crawled out of his shanty and looked out over the junkyard community in which he lived—if it could be called living—with the others who refused to follow the Ra. All told, there was perhaps fifty members of this little garbage village. It used to be bigger, but one by one the residents had died off or given up resistance in exchange for the marks on their foreheads and palms.

Zach had vowed to himself and the others of the village he would never get the mark. The Ra were false; he would never give up his faith in the one true God to follow something so empty.

The fact that the Ra was telling Earth there were no true gods, that they themselves had been mistaken for gods in Earth's past, raised many red flags. He knew the scriptures: Satan could disguise himself as a child of light. If anyone told of a gospel other than that of Christ, that gospel was false. Their words tried to discredit Jesus as savior of the world and Son of God. It trivialized Christianity, calling it a mere misunderstanding of ancient people. Zach could not follow such doctrine. He would keep faith in his savior Jesus Christ.

He would follow the light of God no matter how deep the surrounding darkness grew. This was Zach's vow every morning as he woke in his garbage-bed. If he was being honest with himself, he would admit the temptation was there, offering him freedom from this dismal life. The Ra's head henchman had visited his little camp just last week. Bob Gulam called himself the Prophet of the Ra. Bob had been friendly, offering escape from their suffering. And for so little! Submit to the Ra and receive their mark of loyalty, that was all!

Zach scoffed as he recalled the visit. The offer had been veiled with a threat. While not saying it outright, Bob had suggested the Ra's patience was not infinite and if one did not receive the mark now, he did not know if they would have that opportunity later.

Zach shivered. Bob was the Prophet of the Ra, but Zach knew his true identity. He was the Antichrist. Some of Zach's number had left that day. Zach knew he would likely never see them again. Some of them had been his friends. It was sad to see them go. If it wasn't for his vision, he would have likely been in a depressed state. But the vision reinvigorated his hope.

He didn't understand it. But he knew the woman was beckoning to him. He needed to go to her. He began to pack his few belongings. He didn't know where he was going. He just knew there was nothing left for him here in the refuse. He had to get to the woman with the dark brown eyes and soon.

CHAPTER 48

Lucifer sat on his throne, reflecting on the last fifty years. Much had been accomplished. He should have been happy, but he was not.

Bob Gulam, First Seeker, Prophet of the Ra, Antichrist, was going throughout the world, doing a standup job. Because of him, JoAnne and Splinter had a never-ending stream of clients. The crowds had been coming for fifty years straight, in droves. Millions had joined his ranks. Millions more were on the way. Things were going according to plan. So why was he so unhappy?

He knew why. It was the whims of the minority, those few who refused his mark. The die-hard believers were a thorn in his side. Of course, one day he would blot them from existence, but not yet. Not until all that were willing to come, came.

Free will was a huge factor in his plan. He wanted as many to come to him of their own volition as possible. It was the only way. Despite his power, he could not force his will upon any man. He could only entice. Bob, his enticer, would have to continue working on those strong-willed souls, wearing them down until they submitted. A few die-hards would never cave. He knew that. And it angered him.

But more importantly—there was the Gatekeeper. *Where was that abomination anyway*? Wherever she was, she was no longer the infant he had tried to sacrifice before. She would now be fifty years old. He made a mental note to no longer consider her a child. She was a full-blown Gatekeeper, a dangerous adversary, and despite his best efforts, Kerry's location remained a mystery. He knew she was out there somewhere. He could feel it. He hated the feeling!

He wanted her found sooner rather than later. The longer he waited, the more powerful she became. And the more powerful she grew, the harder ultimate victory would be. Of course victory would be his regardless, it was his birth-right. Still, he wanted it now! Patience was not one of his virtues.

He rose from his throne and gazed out the window. As far as the eye could see, people streamed to him to be marked. People of every nation flocked to him for relief. He smiled. Little did they know, their relief would be temporary. Even now, some were given over to torture. Demons must feed after all. Among the line of those who came to get the mark, a third of them were re-routed to the great dining hall, there to meet eternal suffering as the demons feasted.

Those who were not re-routed had no knowledge of the sufferings of those who had been. It did no good for them to know. If such a discovery was made, it would make Bob's job that much more difficult. He didn't want that.

CHAPTER 49

Kerry stood in the Geddon cemetery with a spade in her hands. She looked around as she put the last shovel-full of dirt upon her mother's grave. She was the only funeral attendee above ground. The rest of the town was there—resting in peace six feet under the surface.

She wiped perspiration from her brow. It had not been easy moving her mother's lifeless body, alone, from Matthew's home to the cemetery. The body was dead weight and she was not young.

In fact, this burial process had taken nearly a week. The first day had been the hardest, transporting the body to the grave and putting enough dirt on it to ensure the scavengers stayed away. Then she had left, unable to continue until now.

Loneliness settled in her bones. She wondered who would bury her when she died. But she knew. Nobody would bury her. Her body would lie where it fell. Decay would come slowly in the desert, leaving her to the ravages of mummification unless some predator or scavenger happened to find her first.

What to do now? She wondered. No answer presented itself. She only knew what she could not do. She couldn't leave the last safe place on Earth. She couldn't abandon the ghost town of Geddon. She was the gatekeeper. She didn't know what that meant, but it had to do with the old door in the basement of Matthew's home. She had to stay near that gate and wait for whatever it was she was supposed to wait for.

She thought about life alone in Geddon. She would have no problem surviving here. Her parents had taught her how to live off the land. She knew how to hunt. She knew how to forage. She knew how to grow crops the desert could sustain. Matthew had stockpiled food, water, guns and ammunition. The basement was filled with such provision, from years of accumulation.

Her challenge would be fighting the invisible creature of loneliness. Already, she felt it leaching into her veins and sucking away her vitality. "Please God," she prayed. "Keep me from loneliness. Make me content with this situation. Amen." This was not the first time she had uttered this prayer. It wouldn't be the last.

She wondered what her future entailed. Lonely or not, she was just one middle-aged woman against all the forces of Hell. If the media could be believed, opposition to the Ra was dwindling. Either by promises of a better life, or threats of a horrible existence, many were coming to the Ra and receiving the mark of allegiance. Using the spade as a hammer, she pounded a wooden cross into the newly turned earth that covered her mother's body. She looked at the cross and promised her loyalties would remain firm with the triune God; Father, Son, and Holy Spirit.

She turned her back to the grave, thinking suddenly of the door in the basement. She left the cemetery. Despite her fatigue from transporting and burying her mother, compulsion pushed her to move quickly. She ran down the empty main-street of town. She entered her home and headed down the stairs. She regarded the door hanging upon the wall. She hesitated only momentarily before grabbing the black bulbous-eye of a doorknob. She turned the knob and pulled.

She pulled harder, but nothing changed. The door wouldn't open. This didn't surprise her. The door had been firmly nailed to the wall like the piece of art that it was. Still, she felt this door was meant to be opened by her. The timing was just off. "I'll be patient," she said to it.

Then she laughed. She would never have thought in a million years that she would be talking to doors. Then again, never in her life had she been so lonely.

Someday that door would open. She felt it as intensely as the fact that the door was not meant to open today. She wondered what might come through the door when it was ready to be opened—what might come through and murder her loneliness?

She stared at the door for a long time and studied the black knob. It was shiny and round like an alien eye. She stared. It stared back. *What had her mother said?* She tried to recall. *She was to guard the door until she was a century old, then she would be given knowledge.*

She didn't know what that could possibly mean except that she was scheduled to wait alone for a long time. Again she prayed. "Please God, help me with my loneliness." She was about to say *amen* when she heard something. She strained her ears. Somebody was outside Matthew's home. She was not as alone as she'd thought.

She grabbed her Remington. Usually she used it for obtaining the main ingredient in desert hare stew. Today it had more sinister duties. She put her foot on the first stair that led out of the basement. The stair creaked. She froze.

Outside, she heard voices. They didn't stop when the stair creaked. Confident the intruders had not heard her, she took another step, then another and another. Out of her basement, she stood silent as death. The voices came to her more clearly. She hefted the Remington, and put her hand on her front door's knob. She opened the door.

"Who's there!" she hollered. She zoned in on the intruders and lifted the gun.

*

Zach froze. So did those with him.

"Easy now," he said as calmly as he could. "We're not looking for any trouble."

If he had been asked at that moment to describe who pointed the rifle at his face, he would have failed. However, he could have described the business end of that rifle down to the smallest detail. Silence reigned and time became inconsequential as he stared down that dark tunnel. Only his thudding heart counted off the seconds.

The one with the gun shattered the silence. "State your business."

Zach wished he could see who held the rifle more clearly, but try as he might, he couldn't see beyond the rifle looming before his face.

"I said state your business." The woman's voice came again.

"Tell her Zach," he heard a voice from his group pipe up.

Zach didn't know how or where to begin. "We're looking for the lonely woman." He sounded ridiculous. He closed his eyes, expecting the rifle's report to be the last thing his ears ever registered. He waited. He heard nothing. He opened his eyes.

The rifle was no longer leveled at him. The woman with the rifle was no longer out of focus. She was center stage, holding the weapon such that it could quickly be returned to firing position. The expression on her face was odd. "Who—who are you?"

Zach answered. "We are those who refuse the mark of the Ra."

She relaxed her hold on the rifle.

He dared continue. "We are the unmarked. Seven days ago, I had a vision of a lonely woman. In the vision, you beckoned us, so we came."

"How did you know where to find me?" the woman asked.

Zach shrugged. "We went where we felt we were being led. I know it sounds unbelievable but…"

She interrupted. "Nothing sounds strange to me anymore. How many are you?"

"About forty." He looked back at the ragtag group that had joined him, accepting him as their leader, saddened and grateful at the same time. "Not all of us have survived, but others joined us on the way."

The woman looked beyond them. "Were you followed?"

They had avoided urban areas, traveled by night and taken cover under foliage or in caves or anywhere else they could find during the day. "I don't think so," he said.

She stood there for what seemed to be a long time. "Wait here," she finally said, and disappeared back into the house.

Zach was not sure if they should wait or not. What if the vision was wrong? What if this was some mind-control scheme of the Ra? What if this woman was in their employ? But she reappeared, dragging something big and orange. It took a second for him to realize what she had. "A thermos?" he asked in disbelief. By the way she moved, he could tell it was not empty.

She filled a cup from the thermos and handed it to Zach.

He put it to his lips. It was water. It tasted wonderful.

Soon all of them were taking turns drinking and the thermos was filled again and again until their dehydration had been quenched. It was the best day Zach could remember since the good old days when the unmarked were still considered to have rights.

PART THREE

Seeker's Salvation Day - plus 100 years

CHAPTER 50

*

"And I stood upon the sand of the sea, and saw a beast rise up out of the sea, having seven heads and ten horns, and upon his horns ten crowns, and upon his heads the name of blasphemy. And the beast which I saw was like unto a leopard, and his feet were as the feet of a bear, and his mouth as the mouth of a lion; and the dragon gave him power, and his seat and great authority. And I saw one of his heads as it were wounded to death and his deadly wound was healed." – Revelation 13:1-3.

*

Deep in the wastelands of Outer Earth, the hundred-year-old egg began to shiver. It was Osiris' shift.

Osiris was melancholy up to that point. He had wished to be in the number that had crossed The Space Between. Instead, he had been assigned, along with the rest of his detachment, guard duty

He knew Lucifer took joy in his disappointment, which only frustrated him further. But there was little to be done. The egg had to be guarded. That was the order, which he must obey under pain of severe punishment. They repeatedly drove off the pathetic attempts of the man Hunter. It was a dull job, far too easy with the power Lucifer had left them, which only added to his boredom.

Now however, Osiris' mood changed as he babysat his charge. He watched the egg intently, at first disbelieving his senses. Then it shivered again, more violently than before. There could be no doubt. The time of the hatching had arrived.

The shivering of the egg grew until it shook the land and sprayed desert sand into the air around it. Osiris took a tentative step back as the shell cracked. Bits of shell pinged off his armor. He took a second step away.

Through the crack, black smoke plumed, smelling of sulfur. It reminded him of the bowels of his home, Hades. He inhaled the fumes and felt content wash over him. He exhaled it back out of his demonic lungs like one enjoying a fine cigar.

The crack widened. The smoke grew thicker. Osiris took another drag, and nearly fainted with the intoxication of it all. He stumbled backwards, tripping over his own feet as the shell disintegrated into an explosion of shards and noxious gas. Shell bits found the spaces between his armor plates and stuck into his flesh as the shock wave hit him. He didn't mind the shrapnel. It was a small price to pay for being present during this prophecy's fulfillment.

The smoke had grown so thick he couldn't see more than a few inches in front of him. His damned heart pounded with excitement. He was not alone. This he knew. He could feel the other's presence. It was close. It was wonderful. The beast had hatched. In his exuberance, he couldn't tell how much time had passed.

As the smoke cleared, a dark silhouette formed within the haze. The shadows of seven heads took shape. He could see them flailing about on spindly necks. Six were long and thin. The seventh was not. The seventh was thick, wounded and healed, just as the prophecy foretold.

Without hesitation, one of the snakelike heads shot upward. It disappeared in the sky where the Space Between separates the Earths. Osiris cackled with glee. After all, the hatchling would need to feed to build up its strength and it would need a lot of strength for its mission.

He grinned as he thought of all the souls that would have to die for the beast to feast, and danced a happy jig, cackling all the while.

CHAPTER 51

Marcy had stood in line for what seemed an eternity. Still, those who had requested her presence had been kind enough as she waited and waited and waited. The Ra made sure she was well-fed and provisioned as she waited in line to receive the mark. Their generosity made her feel better about her decision. She had struggled a long time on whether to commit to the Ra. Now she wondered why she hadn't done it sooner.

The Ra had been exceedingly friendly. Of course friendliness is relative. Before her decision to convert, she'd been living in squalor because of them. She'd been jobless, perpetually hungry, tired, nearly naked for lack of clothing, and generally discriminated against. But that was all before her life-changing decision. Now the crap of life was behind her, she was sure of it.

It had taken her a while. Like a recovering addict, she'd had to hit rock bottom. There, she found only a void—where she'd hoped to find God, she discovered instead that no God existed. The only gods were the Ra.

That's when she realized the offer still stood for redemption, if only she would receive the mark. So she renounced the existence of the God of her ancestors. It was like ripping off a Band-Aid. The anticipation was excruciating, but once done she realized it wasn't as bad as she'd feared.

Now, however, she felt antsy. She hadn't yet received the mark and was no longer in line to receive it. Some of the Ra had pulled her from her place. She'd worried that somehow it had been determined she was not worthy of the mark, but they explained that, on the contrary, she was being honored; separated into a smaller group, a special group. Marcy couldn't believe it. Even after she had resisted for so long, they accepted her not only as one of the flock, but someone to be privileged!

They escorted her along with the other unmarked 'specials' to a secluded portion of the compound. The group was small, only three others. She glanced covertly at them as they were bustled along to their 'special' accommodations. As a group, they appeared proud as peacocks. Her old religion would have said pride cometh before a fall, but that was old jargon. It didn't apply to her any more. *Why not pride?* she asked herself. *It's not every day an alien race deems you a cut above the rest.*

Her sufferings were over! She would no longer live in dumps. She would no longer go hungry. She would no longer have to eek her way through life. She was now under the protection of the Ra. In exchange, her loyalty to them would be absolute.

She passed by others as they were bustled along. All of those she passed were either Ra, or had received their mark. She felt strangely naked without her mark. *Patience, Marcy, just a little while longer and the mark will be upon you.*

Two Ra led their group of four and two more brought up the rear. She looked at them. The Ra all shared the same traits. The men were handsome and muscular, the women athletic and beautiful. The exception was their leader. Lucifer was handsome and muscular, yet she couldn't look at him. He repelled her, despite his looks. Perhaps he was too much of a good thing?

Marcy rallied her courage "Where are we going?" she asked one of her Ra chaperones.

He didn't turn, but uttered. "To the feast."

Marcy felt fear at the sound of his voice. She didn't understand why. The Ra were her new benefactors. They were benevolent gods. Why should she fear them? She pushed herself to speak again. "What kind of feast?"

"A beast feast," was his answer.

Marcy thought on this. Her family were known as excellent hunters. That was one of the reasons they had survived so long without the mark. When the game had been plentiful, her family had often had beast feasts with other hunters—big get-togethers where the kills were prepared and eaten and shared. It was not until the wild game was gone that her family began to truly suffer.

She wondered what kind of beasts were being prepared for them today. She was sure it would be something special. After all, they were *privileged* members of the Union of the Ra. They were specials.

Truth be told, she wasn't picky. She'd been living off rats and crows for years. She thought of the feast to come. She was so hungry. Even though she'd been rescued by the Ra from her life of poverty, she hadn't yet fully pulled her body from the ravages of years of near-starvation. Her mouth watered. Her stomach growled. She relished the feast to come.

CHAPTER 52

Kerry wasn't sure where she was. It was a strange place; a strange city filled with strange inhabitants. The strangeness of it suggested she was dreaming. The people (if they were people) were exceedingly tall and unnaturally pale. She saw in her dream-state that they were frantic, panicked. She could hear them. They spoke a strange language, yet she understood them. They were desperately trying to secure the city, preparing for a great and imminent battle.

She tried to catch every word that came from their lips. She must know what it was they were preparing to battle against. But there were too many voices. Then, with one monstrous roar, the answer became clear. The roar was so great it shook the city and those within its walls. The tall people froze in fear.

Kerry shuddered at the great and terrible sound. Her belief that she was dreaming did nothing to quell her fears. She sought the source of the roar, and when she saw it, her courage evaporated. It was a beast like no other. Its head was like a dragon's. Protruding from it were other, lesser heads. These heads resembled eyeless snakes as they flailed about the greater dragon-head like the serpent-hairs of Medusa. It roared again. She had never known a sound to be in itself, evil. But this roar was.

As she gazed upon the abomination, she saw those in the city would not be able to stop it. It was too powerful. In her dream, she shouted at the city-dwellers. "Run! It's your only chance! Run to the door! Run!"

*

Kerry jolted awake and fell from her bed. Hitting the ground, she screamed. The scream ended abruptly as she realized the beast had stayed behind in the nightmares. At the same time, a dark revelation descended upon her with such force she dared not disbelieve it. The strange city was real, as were its inhabitants. The beast was real and as evil as she had seen in her dream. That last thought made her cry.

The second revelation was this: they could not fight this evil. They would have to flee. In her dream she had yelled out for those fleeing to run to the door. An image of the yellow door with the coal-black knob popped into her mind. *So, my door would be the means of escape.*

She pulled her ancient bones off the bedroom floor. She must act quickly.

CHAPTER 53

Marcy waited in the room with the others of the 'special, yet to be marked' sect. Their Ra escorts had left them there. The room was simple. There were no furnishings of any kind, no windows. A drain was in the center of the floor, like those on the floor of any average public restroom. Light shone down from a large skylight overhead. It hardly seemed a place for a feast. Surely it was just a stopping point.

She sat down on the hard, carpet-free floor, resting her back against a wall. Her stomach growled, reminding her of her hunger, and of the promised feast. She tried not to dwell on her pangs, but it was a losing battle. She was still ascending from the pit of poverty in which she had existed for so long.

She stroked her long hair. It was so smooth, so silky, so clean. She was not used to clean hair until recently. Now, she stroked it when feeling on edge. Such actions calmed her.

Despite the mercy the Ra had extended, she felt uneasy. Those who had escorted them into the room had seemed to possess a hunger all their own despite appearing well-fed. She suspected their hunger went deeper than an empty stomach. She was relieved when they left.

She glanced at the others in the room. They all looked as she did. Of course they did. They'd all come from the same background, vowing loyalty to the Ra after years of poverty and discrimination. Like her, they sat on the ground with their backs against the walls. Like her they all had a look of hunger. None of them spoke. Together, they waited for the promised feast.

Marcy's eyes drifted around the room. She wondered about the purpose of the drain. It put her further on edge. Something else slowly dawned on her. The entrance to the room, through which they had been escorted, was a one-way door. She remembered a knob on the far side which one of the Ra had used to enter. There was no knob on this side. Her edginess grew as she looked for an alternate exit and saw none. The room suddenly felt small, or perhaps she felt very large.

Then the noise began—a humming from above. She looked up. The skylight was opening. She had not realized how stuffy the room had grown until then. Fresh air replaced the stale, but did nothing to ease Marcy's fears. The skylight continued to open. The humming continued to hum. Her edginess persisted and festered.

The skylight opened further. Her heart thudded like a drum. The taunt skin on her white-knuckled fists appeared on the verge of tearing. Unintentionally, she whimpered. The humming stopped. The skylight was now fully open.

She began to stroke her hair with renewed vigor; it did nothing to ease her mind. Her edginess persisted and festered.

CHAPTER 54

Kerry stood before the yellow door and stared the black knob directly in the eye. The door needed to be opened. The dream had told her so. It was the only escape for the strange people in the strange city who were being attacked by the beast.

She put her hundred-year-old hand on the coal-black knob and stared down the door like an old west gunslinger preparing for a high-noon showdown. She wanted to turn the knob, yet she hesitated. It was overwhelming. It was a door to nowhere and should not have the ability to be opened, or if it did, it would only open to a bare basement wall.

On the other hand, her life had been pumped full of memories about things that happened that defied logic. Why would that change now? Still, she hesitated in turning that knob.

Everything seemed frozen in time as she stood there, a hundred-year-old woman, willing herself to do something that logic dictated would be only a non-event. Her eyes narrowed further as the showdown commenced.

In her mind, she could hear the screams of the strange people in the strange city as the beast ravaged them. They were the cries of many, yet they bombarded her in unison as if they shrieked out from one giant mouth.

The screams upset her, but not as much as the vicious noise of the beast that overwhelmed all else. That evil, blasphemous sound haunted her still. She broke through her hesitation. She turned the knob.

CHAPTER 55

What started as a whimper grew to a shriek. The shriek cut short. Then silence. Abe, one of the elite who had been escorted into the small, windowless room, had been told a feast was coming. Now he understood.

Terror filled him as the shrieker ceased shrieking. This was the girl who had been stroking her hair. He felt a scream rise in his own throat. But terror bottled it up, his larynx unable to release it. He watched, unable to turn away, though he desperately wanted to. This poor woman's demise mesmerized him.

A great eyeless snake-like creature had slammed into her from the open skylight above. It smashed her skull and lit her up like a Halloween pumpkin. He watched as her arms flailed in a gruesome display. The stench of brains on the griddle permeated the air. The thing throbbed as it fed, sucking up the desired morsels. Abe tried to tell himself it was fake. It couldn't really be happening. But deep down he knew what he saw was no illusion.

He heard a pounding. Abe turned towards it. It was one of the others. The man's face was distorted with horror and Abe figured it mirrored his own. He banged on the door, searching for the non-existent knob. He screamed as he pounded, pleading for mercy, begging to be released, but no response came from the other side of the door.

And Abe understood. It fell into place like tumblers in a lock. The Ra had left them in this inescapable cell and opened the skylight. The Ra had let in the killing thing that was now finishing off the woman. The Ra had put a drain in the room for one reason: convenient clean-up.

"Oh crap!" *The thing was finishing with the hair-stroker. Who's next?*

The snake backed out of the smoking corpse. It turned! It turned towards Abe! He closed his eyes. He hoped for a painless end.

A brief gargled scream made him open his eyes. The snake had taken out the one at the door. And now there were only two. Abe watched as the other fainted. As if it could sense weakness, the snake went for the fainter. It made short work of that one. Now, only Abe remained. His time was up. He closed his eyes once again fully expecting it to be the last time.

CHAPTER 56

Bob Gulam was ecstatic as he rode along in the transport. As prophet of the Ra, he held the highest status. Therefore he rode in the cockpit with the pilot. The entire transport was filled with converts who would soon receive their marks. He looked out the window as they flew and saw far below, the vast ocean.

These converts marked a milestone for Bob. They had been found on a remote island, the most remote island, the last speck of earth he had not yet visited.

This meant the entire world had been given the message. His job, which he'd been doing for a century now, was at an end. He thought what this meant for him. He barely remembered the days before he had been the messenger of the Ra. The days of being the First Seeker seemed no more than the distant dream of a long-past memory.

He grinned. Now the world had received the message down to the last known human being, the next phase in Lucifer's plan could begin: the elimination of the small pockets of people so closed-minded they refused Bob's message of mercy and grace. It would be, in the tradition of Adolf Hitler, "the final solution." Finally, the purification of the human race could begin. Unlike Hitler's solution, the extermination would not be based on race, nationality, or sexual orientation, but on failure to wear the marks.

Bob's grin widened as he thought of the additional prize that waited in the transport along with those who were to receive the mark. This other prize was not a convert, but information that came to him as the result of an execution. On the island, there had been a small band of people who had not chosen to give up their superstitious ideas about god, foolishly rejecting the Ra's offer.

This was nothing unusual. Normally, a few resisted. What was unusual was a map that one of the rebels had—a map of southern California. *Why would an isolated islander of the Pacific Rim have a map of southern California?* More strangely still, the map was hand-made. Yet it was so detailed that Bob had no doubt as to what it was.

This was a primitive people who lived in isolation from the rest of the world. Their culture had not even been discovered until shortly before the arrival of the Ra. Unfortunately, they had been discovered by a group of

Christian missionaries which made Bob's job that much more difficult. Even though a century had passed since these primitives had converted to Christianity, their faith had not weakened over the decades.

Bob had been sure this man had never been to Southern California. So, how did he draw the map? That was the million dollar question. He needed answers and he had the ability to get them. Lucifer had given him such authority.

The interrogation had gone poorly at first. The man simply babbled of his ridiculous faith in Jesus Christ, calling the Ra false gods. He even tried to witness to Bob in hopes he could persuade him to become a Christian—as if that were even possible!

None of this was unusual. Those who refused to accept the way of the Ra always claimed the Ra were false. But that map—that map was the flawed numeral in an otherwise sound equation.

As he flew along in the cockpit of the transport, Bob thought on that map. It had an X on it in the middle of the California desert, and beside the X, the word *Geddon.* Bob had checked all records. There was no town named Geddon in California. No map acknowledged it except for this one the man had created on an island that should have no knowledge of such places. *A mystery.*

Bob didn't like mysteries. So, he cracked the one that held the secret and coerced him to talk. Under what Bob classified as intense questioning, though others may have deemed it torture, the man talked, but his answers only deepened the mystery.

He had been having dreams of a hundred-year-old woman who lived in a place called Geddon, California. She was begging him to come to her for sanctuary from the Ra. In his dreams, she stood before a great door. The door was yellow with a black knob. The woman's name was Kerry.

This was vague. Bob had wanted more, but the man refused to say more even under threat of greater torture. Instead, he forgave Bob for what he had done to him as well as for what he may still do. That was the last thing he ever uttered. Greater torture silenced him forever.

Now, in the cockpit of the transport, Bob reported to his master all he had learned. On the communicator, Lucifer had not sounded overly interested until the mention of the old woman's name. Upon hearing it, he became very interested.

Lucifer gave two commands to Bob. The second command was to quickly transport the map back to Ra headquarters. The first was to kill the one who had drawn the map. With the second soon to be done and the first already accomplished, Bob relaxed in the cockpit beside the pilot. It had been a good day.

CHAPTER 57

Hunter fumed as he thought on his failure to destroy the egg. His failure however was not for lack of trying. He had ventured back multiple times to where the egg was, but realized quickly that destroying the egg would be suicide. Demons guarded it day and night. Even with his power of five, he stood no chance of getting near enough to destroy it.

And now the beast had hatched and was wrecking havoc on the great city of Outer Earth. Hunter alone stood to confront it as it penetrated the outer defenses. Nora, Moses, and the rest had retreated. Hunter thought on this and shuddered.

Of course he wanted it this way. His son especially had wanted to stand his ground beside him, but Hunter would not allow it. Standing ground against the beast was suicide for everyone but him. And even for Hunter, the odds were, like in Vegas, strongly in favor of the house.

The all-too-familiar roar permeated his ears as the beast drew nearer. The fearful sound eroded his courage. Still, he stood strong. His power was not his own. God had helped him defeat the beast once before and only by His will would he be able to defeat it twice.

The beast laughed maliciously as one of its slender serpent-heads flew upward and penetrated The Space Between. Hunter knew this meant it was feeding. It would soon be stronger.

*

Otis sat on his throne. More precisely, Otis sat around his throne. Otis was a man of carriage—or, to those less kind, a lard-ball. He called himself big-boned. In reality, he was just plain fat. Of course, no one ever said that to his face, not to Otis.

Otis was a high-ranking member of the Union of the Ra. He had proven his loyalty and been rewarded with a territory to rule. The Scottish Highlands were his domain. As Governor of the region, he was to ensure that those with the mark receive their due rations and those without the mark receive their due discrimination.

He sat alone in his judgment chamber, a glass of fine wine in his hand. Life was good for Otis. The sun had recently set. He smiled, thinking of his day. He had received word from Lucifer: the time of toleration was at an end. It was time to tell those without the mark that it was do or die. He relished the opportunity to eliminate those who refused the Ra. He relished it like the fine wine he sipped.

His throne faced the large panoramic window to his hilltop estate. From here, he could see for miles, keeping his eyes on his subjects. Beyond his vision existed the slums where those without the mark lived a pitiful existence. He was glad such eyesores were beyond his ability to see from his window and happier still they would soon be no more.

He rose from his throne. It was no graceful rising, but filled with huffing and puffing. Once up, he waddled to the window, squinting into the sky. He thought he'd seen lightning, but lighting was unusual for this time of year, leaving him unsure. He stared intently into the night sky, searching.

What happened next caught Otis off guard. The eyeless snake slammed through the glass of his viewing window. Glittery shards stabbed into his blubbery flesh. Flying glass bit into him, showered him, but he barely noticed. His skull had been shattered and his soul was being harvested.

For a moment, Otis' flabby body jiggled like oobleck on an upturned stereo speaker. His fat fist released the glass of wine which shattered on the floor in a puddle of red. Then the tub of blubber that had been Otis plopped to the ground as if the plug had been yanked on the stereo.

Otis was dead. He no longer had to worry about seeing the disgusting inhabitants of the unmarked population or deal with their demise. He now had other worries. His soul now faced new terrors, unimaginable terrors.

*

The beast drew closer to Hunter. The snake-head retracted back into this side of the Space Between. It was bloody, very bloody, as if it had just skewered a whale. A chunk of blubber dangled from the tip.

Hunter could wait no longer. *One, two, three, four five*, he chanted as he flew at his enemy with five times the strength of a normal man. He slammed into the creature, repulsed by the feel of it. The ugly sensation of the contact penetrated deep into his soul. He couldn't back away; his momentum committed him.

The creature seemed to absorb him as they connected, as if he sank into a deep pillow, engulfed by downy stuffing—except it was not comforting. It was horrifying. He struggled to pull himself out.

The beast tumbled backwards. Hunter bounced away like a pinball off a bumper. He landed on the ground, skidding across the ground like a plane hitting the runway with no landing gear. A plume of Outer Earth dust rooster-tailed behind him.

By the time both bodies skidded to a halt, they were a hundred feet apart. A thousand wouldn't have been far enough for Hunter's liking. He scrambled up, seeing his enemy toppled onto its side and struggling to regain its feet. Hunter seized the moment, driving in for another attack.

One, two, three, four, five! He flew at the beast. He noticed, as he did, that the blasphemies normally coming from the creature had diminished. He could still hear them, but not as intensely as before the collision. A sign of weakness? He hoped so.

It struggled vainly to rise. He had injured it! He shot into the melee of flailing serpent heads, dodging as they whipped about. They seemed to have lost purpose and become unaware of him. The beast howled as if in agony.

Hunter had no mercy. It deserved none except for the mercy to be put out of its misery. He had no weapon but the power of five. It would have to be enough.

He skidded to a stop just feet from the creature's head. Through the hole in its neck, it gasped for air. A rattling sound emanated from it. The beast let out a moan and something resembling a cough. Its eyes appeared glassy before closing. They did not reopen.

Hunter leapt into the air as he counted. The death punch would be glorious. He leapt high over the beast and descended, ready to pound the beast between the eyes. At this speed, God had surely given him victory. His blow would fracture the giant skull. Fifty feet became forty in the blink of an eye—twenty-five—fifteen—five—*slam!*

The connection was made, but not as he had envisioned. One of the eyeless snake-heads shot from behind and shafted into his lower back. Hunter looked down, seeing himself impaled. Shock wavered in his brain, not comprehending. He felt no pain, only an icy sensation where the beast and he had united in unholy matrimony. Slowly his brain caught up. Lethargically, it registered what had happened.

Hunter heard laughter. He felt it as well. It came from the beast, vibrating through their shared connection. Wordlessly, the beast spoke. Hunter understood: his enemy had been playing possum. He knew its intentions. It would destroy Outer Earth and make it its own. Then, it would cross the Space Between to help usher in the never-ending reign of Lucifer.

All was lost. It sank into Hunter's thoughts. The icy cold left him. The pain hit. He shrieked. The beast laughed harder. The pain increased. Hunter prayed to Jesus for death. Strangely enough, his last thought was that the beast had made a mistake. He was not the last obstacle in the enemy's way. He was but one servant. God had many more.

    Hunter died.

CHAPTER 58

As Kerry turned the knob, the door flew open with such force her arm nearly came from its socket. It sent her spiraling to the far side of the basement. She sprawled, uninjured as far as she could tell, with a dull roar in her ears. It seemed to be a throng of voices all speaking at once in an indecipherable language, with the power of rushing rapids.

She stared at the door in amazement. It was wide open. Behind it, where there should have been the white-painted masonry of the house's foundation, was, instead, a seething, seemingly living thing. It bulged into the basement like overflowing mucus, then retreated as if sucked away from the open door, then oozed in again like a tide.

The goo was without color; its depth appeared infinite. The noise permeated the basement, loudest when the goo protruded towards her.

At those moments, she could almost make out the individual voices from the shouting throng. They were the fearful screams of people in great distress. Over the screams another voice rose, a horrible voice. As recognition struck her, she shivered in terror. This was the voice of the beast.

She cowered into the furthest corner of the room not knowing what she could do to escape that which was coming for her through the opening. Then she remembered the others from her dream—the tall, pale people. They needed to escape, before it was too late.

Despite her fear, she forced herself into action. She stood up. She approached the doorway. She tried to anticipate what might come through, but she had no idea at all.

CHAPTER 59

The last survivors of Outer Earth huddled in the inner-most room of the inner-most building of what remained of the once-great city. It was now a city of ruins, a town of death.

Terror filled Nora. Although her son had escaped the beast once before, it seemed an escape that was unlikely to be repeated. She looked at Moses. She had watched him grow into a young man; strong, handsome, and full of faith. Now his life was in jeopardy. He had inherited his father's OCD, but not the power of five. Without that, how did he stand any chance against this foe?

The roar of the beast echoed far away as it hunted outside. They were the last of its prey. She looked around the room in which they hid. It was an average space in an average building like so many others that had once existed in the great city, yet this particular room seemed to hold special significance.

The beast roared again. It sounded nearer. Time was flittering away.

There were not many in the room, only a handful crammed into the hiding place with her and Moses, like sardines in a tin, she and Moses dwarfed by the pale giants of Outer Earth. She shivered in this forest of albino trees, fearing the death that awaited them.

The roar of the beast boomed again, closer now, perhaps just outside the door. It was close enough she caught a hint of its blasphemies.

A slippery thought slithered her mind, making her heart race, her breath quicken, her muscles tense. *Hunter had failed! Ergo, Hunter was dead!* It hit her like a bomb but it had to be true. If Hunter was alive, the beast would not have made it this far into the city.

Her gut tied itself into knots as that knowledge dug talons deep inside her. She was now a widow, her only solace that they would all soon be together in paradise. Yes, it would be very soon, she conjectured.

Despite her sorrow, she forced herself to a comparative calm. She put her hope in the afterlife and in her God who had promised it to her. With the calm came another realization. She remembered why this room was special.

It was the room she had first entered into through the Space Between so long ago. Coincidence? No. Experience had taught her nothing occurs by coincidence. Everything that happens is by God's design. Despite her predicament, she smiled. Her time here had come full-circle. It seemed she had arrived back at the beginning.

Suddenly, a bright light blazed. She flinched. A door appeared where none had been. Her mouth gaped. She recognized the yellow door with the black knob. It didn't seem possible, but there it was: Nancy's door!

This development was bitter-sweet. Salvation had come for all but one.

*

In unison Moses and the others turned to the doorway. Moses knew what it was. They all knew. His parents had described the yellow door with the black knob before, when telling how they came to be in Outer Earth.

The door opened. The Space Between beckoned them.

Without hesitation, the ones closest entered the opening. Normally such a stoic people would hesitate, but not now, not when it was their only hope. He felt his mother's hand on his shoulder. "You're going home, son," she whispered.

Uneasiness settled in his bones as he corrected her. "We're both going home."

She shook her head. "Not all of us."

His pulse quickened.

"Not me," she added.

He turned to her, trying to keep tears at bay. He failed. The tears flowed. "Of course you're coming," he said.

"I can't," she said. "It's a one-time, one-way ticket and it's a ticket I've already redeemed."

Moses' lungs seemed unable to fill with air. He looked at the portal. Already half of the inhabitants of the room were gone. Outer Earth was nearly deserted.

He looked back at his mother. He would not let her hang on this ridiculousness. She would come with them. He would force her if need be! He grabbed her, pulling. She resisted.

"Come on!" he screamed.

"It will do no good, Moses!" she shouted.

Outside the room, the beast roared, drawn by their scuffle.

"Please!" he begged. "There's no time!"

She planted her feet. "I can't go back!"

"If you can't, neither can I! I came from the same world you did remember?"

She shook her head. "No, you came here in the womb, but you were born an outer earthling. You *can* go back. You must!"

Moses looked once again at the portal, it was still open. They were the only ones left.

She kissed him on the cheek and tried to pull away. He refused to let her, clinging to her as if she was life itself!

With a boom, the wall opposite the doorway disintegrated. The dust settled. The beast peered in.

Moses prepared to fight, but before he could attack, his mother slammed him into the portal. The last thing he saw as he entered the space between was the beast attacking.

His mother was no more.

CHAPTER 60

Kerry stared at the door in disbelief. Tall, pale beings popped from the open doorway as if falling off a conveyor-belt. These were the people of her dream, now crowding into her basement in stark reality. She hoped they would stop popping into the room before space ran out.

Her first thought was to bring towels. They were covered with the goo of the stuff within the doorway. Many were scraping the stuff off, leaving it in wet piles at their feet. A few shook like wet dogs trying to get dry.

The newcomers stared at her. She couldn't tell if they were happy, sad, frightened or otherwise. She could only describe them as stoic. Being too tall for the low basement, they hunched over her with analytical stares. She returned their gaze with one of her own. These giants looked powerful as she stood beneath them, a frail hundred-year-old woman. Yet despite their size, she sensed a collective gentleness of spirit.

A loud noise drew her attention. It sounded like a whip had been snapped just inches from her ear. She turned just in time to see the door disintegrate. In its place, on the floor beneath where the door had once been, was a mess of yellow dust. Half-buried in the pile was a glossy black something. She looked harder. Recognition hit. It was the cracked orb of the coal-black knob.

The last one who had made it through the door stood there shivering. He was also covered in goo, but neither scraped it off nor shook it free. She saw his terror; unlike the others, she could read his expression. Whether it was his sorrow, or that he lacked their height and paleness, she felt drawn to this last newcomer. She wanted to console him. She wanted to stop his shivers of terror. She opened her mouth to speak. Words failed her.

*

The story of Jonah and the whale popped into Moses' head. For as Jonah was vomited from the fish and unwillingly led to Nineveh, so too he had been vomited through the door and unwillingly led to Inner Earth. The first thing he noticed was how small the space was in which they found themselves. Being from the land of giants, low-ceilinged spaces were rare. He looked at his fellow refugees from a place that was now the haunt of demons and beasts.

Within the packed space, he saw another. She was aged and stooped, with a long, thick, gray braid. She studied him with an intensity that should have made him uncomfortable, but did not. Strangely, he felt a connection to this woman, although they had never met. How could they have, being from opposite sides of the Space Between? Maybe it was because she was like him. He had never seen another of his own race, besides his parents. But she was old—older than anyone he had ever seen.

He looked her over from the bottom of her gnarled feet to the top of her gray head as well as everything in-between. She looked so small, so fragile, surrounded by Outer Earthlings, so tiny.

He forced himself to break the mesmerizing atmosphere this old lady created. He looked back, hoping what he had seen before being thrown from his world was not true. But there was no longer a door on this side of the space between—just a pile of dust and a black shiny something. There was no sign of his mother and he knew: his last sight of his old world was no illusion. His mother was dead.

He bent over, and picked up the glossy-black knob from the pile of yellow dust. It was cold in his hand, reminding him of death. He let it fall again. It landed with a clank upon the floor. He looked back at the old woman. She took a step closer and for the first time, he glimpsed her eyes. They were such a deep brown, a haunting deep brown. He found consolation in the depths of those murky orbs. At the same time, he felt the odd connection between them deepen. Without knowing why, he reached for her. She stepped into him. They embraced. Together they cried.

CHAPTER 61

"Geddon California?" Lucifer inquired.

"Yes, my Lord," Bob answered.

"Geddon California," Lucifer said again.

Bob nodded. He had presented the map to his master. He hoped it would please him. So far, it seemed it had.

"Does this location show up on any other maps?"

"Not to my knowledge," Bob said. "It is a place of mystery."

Lucifer shook his head. "There is no mystery here. This is where the Gatekeeper has been hiding all these years. Of this, I am certain."

Bob nodded again. He didn't understand what was being said, but he dared not ask questions; such questions might spark the wrath of his master. He didn't want that.

Lucifer smiled broadly. "We must attack Geddon and defeat the Gatekeeper. And not only her but those who have sided with her. Geddon will be a cursed name." His eyes gleamed. "We will wipe it from existence."

Bob nodded again. Lucifer looked him in the eyes. Direct eye contact made Bob sweat.

"I'll need a second in command when I rule this world."

Bob trembled. The direct eye contact in conjunction with what he was saying was overwhelming.

"Over the course of the last century, you have shown your faithfulness to the Ra as well as to me."

Bob wondered if he was hearing correctly. Was he actually be commended by Lucifer? It seemed he was. A rare event.

"Once Geddon is in our hands, I will give you a reward befitting your loyalty."

Bob smiled, though he still hardly dared believe his ears. In all of his years seeking, and later knowing, the Ra, he had never experienced such honor.

"But first, we will double-insure our victory. Go get the one the beast spared. I have a purpose for him."

Lucifer told Bob the plan for the one the beast spared and Bob hurried from his presence before Lucifer could change his mind. He went after Abe.

CHAPTER 62

Abe sat in the room with the drain below and the skylight above. He had gone through many phases: terror, shock, disbelief, and finally acceptance. For a good while, he sat scrunched, pulled into himself with his eyelids pinched closed, but in the silence, he opened them carefully.

Cadavers littered the room, oozing fluid through gaping holes in their skulls. Tendrils of crimson flowed from where they had fallen to the floor-drain that drank it up. No one survived but him. He had no idea why he had been spared.

He looked at his hand, where the mark of the Ra should have been. Its absence frustrated him. Had they deemed him unworthy? Would he have been better off staying away from the Ra altogether? Perhaps he should have remained as he had been, an outcast of society—one of the unmarked.

His nerves trembled. The Ra were a power not to be trifled with. It was why he had finally given up resistance. A sense of being watched hit him. He spun.

Standing in the open door was the man who had recruited him—the great prophet of the Ra he had once considered to be the Antichrist. The unsettling feeling grew as the prophet stepped into the room.

"Abe," he said. "What happened to your companions?" He looked about as if the bodies were nothing but piles of garbage.

Abe tried to speak, but no words came. The prophet's indifference to these dead stunned him.

"It looks like you alone have been deemed worthy to live," he said with a grin. "Count yourself lucky, friend. Not many who are escorted into this room are granted such mercies."

Abe remained silent. The prophet drew closer, circling slowly around him. The sadistic grin on the man's face suggested maybe Abe was right in the beginning. Perhaps this prophet of the Ra was indeed the Antichrist.

He nudged one of the corpses out of his path as he circled. "You are a worthy follower of the Ra. I suspected that the moment I laid eyes on you and I suspected you felt the same the moment you heard my message. These suspicions have been confirmed. You are, after all, still among the living."

Abe still did not respond. He turned as the other circled slowly about like some bird of prey zeroing in on a succulent morsel.

The prophet stopped circling and stared into Abe's eyes. "Let's cut to the chase, shall we? The Ra is merciful to whom they choose to show mercy. They spared you." He glanced at the bodies on the floor. "These others—they were not worthy. They got what they deserved. They were only feigning loyalty."

Abe backed away a step, but the prophet eliminated the space between them with a step of his own. "You passed the test Abe."

Abe didn't like where this was going. He didn't understand how he differed from the others. Like them, he had only joined the Ra to escape poverty.

"They spared you, but mercy comes at a cost."

Abe felt ill. Now, he guessed, the truth was coming.

"Lucifer himself has sent me to collect the fee."

Abe's throat felt dry as the desert. What more could Lucifer demand of him? He had already taken everything away.

The prophet seemed to enjoy Abe's misery. "Lucifer himself has sent me to brief you on your mission."

"A mission?" Abe finally found words.

The other nodded. "Once the mission is complete, your debt will be considered paid in full and you will be worthy to receive the mark of the Ra."

"What do I have to do?"

"You are to infiltrate the enemy in their stronghold of Geddon California."

"As a spy?"

The other shook his head. "No, as an assassin."

That word shook Abe to his core. He was a lot of things, but he was no killer.

"You will do as you are commanded, soldier," the other uttered as if he had been able to read Abe's thoughts. "Yes, I call you a soldier because that is what you are."

"No." Abe shook his head.

Before he stopped shaking it, he fell. A strike from the prophet's fist seared him with pain! It connected hard, toppling him to the ground.

One of the bodies broke his fall and he found himself face to face with the hollowed out skull of the other. Blood-soaked hair was matted to that skull, hair once stroked but no more. He scurried off of the corpse like a spider and cowered in the corner, praying for mercy.

The prophet towered over Abe, furious.

Abe wanted to fight, but this was the Ra's prophet. There was no fighting back.

"How dare you defy orders, soldier!" Bob shouted, kicking Abe in the ribs, shouting in delight as Abe cried out in agony.

"If not for the Ra's mercy you would be dead right now!" the prophet shrieked. He turned his rage on one of the dead, kicking the body so hard it burst like an engorged tick. "You would be dead like these others!"

Abe tried to get up, but the prophet kicked him back down. He landed with a moan and curled into a fetal position.

"You want the mark of the Ra?"

In terror, Abe nodded. He would have agreed to just about anything at that moment.

"Well, friend, it's not given for free. You *earn* those marks!"

Abe rolled toward the wall. He just wanted relief.

The prophet grabbed him, hauling him to his feet. Pinned to the wall, the verbal onslaught continued. "That means if the Ra commands you to assassinate somebody, you do it even if they command you to kill your own mother! Do you understand?"

Despite the pain in Abe's ribs, he managed to say yes.

The prophet held him for a moment that felt an eternity. He glared at Abe until the rage seeped away. Then he let go of Abe, letting him slide along the wall back to the floor. "Good. Outside is an incinerator. Take care of this garbage." He gestured at the dead in the room.

For a moment, Abe did not move, but a sharp glance from the other changed that. Despite the pain in his face and ribs, he grabbed the arms of the nearest victim and began to drag it along the floor.

"In the hall closet, you'll find cleaning supplies. Make this room shine." Bob paused and then added, "It has to be presentable for the next group."

With a sadistic smile, the prophet left Abe to his task and his thoughts.

CHAPTER 63

Kerry stood in silence, trying to understand what had been told to her. The story was a bitter pill to swallow. Yet, she believed it. An entire world, an Earth parallel to hers, existed. Even more unfathomable, the place was now a haunt of demons and beasts. The land was not far from her own. She feared her native Earth would soon succumb to an identical fate.

She embraced Moses. He had lost so much. His parents, his life, his entire world, were no more. She felt a connection to this newcomer, as if he were a brother, though he couldn't be. He was, she guessed, about twenty. She was five times that.

She would need to introduce these newcomers to the others of Geddon—so many now. It had started with Zach and his small band of refugees. Then others had trickled in. Over time, the trickle became a flood. All of them had been guided to Geddon by supernatural means; by dreams, visions, and even pulled by unseen arms. Her prayers had been answered. She was no longer a lonely woman. Geddon was no longer a lonely place.

She looked over the newest additions. Besides their appearance, they were no different from the rest; just refugees fleeing the darkness. She remembered what Matthew had told her years back about his dream, how darkness chased them in that dark colored Rogue.

It seemed Geddon was the only place left in the light. She feared the darkness would soon encroach on her town as well. The future of Geddon was in peril.

CHAPTER 64

Abe staggered along the old road, a shadow of what he had been. His hair was disheveled, his eyes were dull, and his gait suggested one much older than his thirty years. No signs existed to tell him if he was going the right direction, but according to the copy of the handmade map that he'd been given, he was heading toward Geddon California. He couldn't reach it soon enough. It was hot. It was dry. He had run out of the meager provisions of water that the Ra had given him. He was miserable.

Still, he was thankful. The Ra had left him alone on the road and he preferred it that way, regardless of how poorly they'd provisioned him. It was as if they didn't care one way or the other if he survived his mission.

His mission: he shook every time he thought of it. He was to infiltrate the enemy where they were strong, in Geddon, and when the time was ripe, assassinate their leader. He disdained it. He was not a murderer. Sure, it had all been explained to him. This was war. He was a soldier following orders.

The description of the leader made his job even more distasteful. Their leader was a woman, a hundred-year-old woman. He would know her by her unusual brown eyes.

He hadn't received the mark of the Ra, so he didn't see how he could be in the army. He would receive it after his mission was complete. It was a mark he no longer wanted, yet one he saw no way of avoiding.

He wondered how he would be received at Geddon. He felt dirty, as if the stench of the Ra was upon him. Would the enemy notice the stench? Would they see him for who he was? A snake in the grass waiting to bite? But he was being fanciful. Of course they couldn't smell the stench of the Ra. It was a stink only he could smell. It leached to him from within.

As he walked the desert road, he had time to plan. *I'll claim to be a defector,* he decided. *If they can tell I come from the Ra, I'll claim to be a defector.* He thought about it as he trudged along. He needed to make sure there were no holes in his strategy. He couldn't think of any, but then, dehydration was hardly conducive to brain activity.

He stared ahead as far as he could see. He strained his eyes until they stung. As he gazed into the distance, the road seemed to take on a life all its own, shimmering and wiggling as if electrified. It was a result of the heat, he told himself; still in his dehydrated state, he wondered.

He wore denim jeans and a long-sleeved shirt. Despite the heat, he refused to remove his clothes. They were the only thing protecting him from the sun. Perhaps it was because the Ra were foreigners to Earth, or maybe they didn't care about their human charges, but they also hadn't provided him with a cover for his head. That, along with the lack of water, played havoc on his body.

He walked on. No, he trudged, his legs barely picking themselves up for the next step, and when they came down, landed haphazardly, chaotically.

With every yard, it became increasingly difficult to keep his path straight. He was unsure if he was unsteady or if the road itself wobbled and veered. Several times, he stumbled into the culvert that hugged either side of the deserted two-lane highway.

The highway itself was hard to follow. Sand dunes covered entire sections and it was clear no one had driven down it for years, maybe even decades. It made sense. Only an abandoned road would lead to a secret city like Geddon.

Something flickered above him. He glanced up, just for a moment. The sun above was too bright for staring. He could only see that something, some *things,* circled above him. Their shadows contrasted darkly against the bright sky. He couldn't tell what they were. He kept walking.

A breeze blew, an unpleasant dry breeze. It blew away what remnants of moisture remained within him. He stumbled. He fell. He rolled into the bone-dry culvert and got a mouthful of sand. He spit out the wad, but a grainy coating stuck to his tongue and refused to leave.

Even when his body settled to a stop, his head continued to spin. His perception danced and wavered, as if he were drunk. He knew dehydration was the mastermind behind his state of being. However, basic thinking was now being trumped by the more primitive attributes indicative of a dying man.

He rolled onto his back, telling himself he would only rest a moment. He looked up into the sky and felt the desert rays bake him.

That strange flickering persisted. He stared hard, no longer caring if the sun burned out his retinas and realized what those strange dark bodies were. They were buzzards. The scavengers circled above him, effortlessly riding the hot-air currents that pushed up from the desert floor. He knew these creatures to be skittish. They would descend to him eventually, when they thought it safe, after he was dead. *Lucky buzzards*, he thought. *They won't be waiting long.*

He would have shed tears at the thought of his impending death, but had no moisture for their creation. Still, he lamented his future which now appeared quite short. He heard a noise. He turned. He saw. *Crap!*

The reptilian face before him appeared larger than life. It flicked a forked tongue. Its eyes were like pearls with elliptical pupils. The image of it shimmered in the desert heat. It took a second for Abe's dehydrated brain to register what he was looking at. At first, he thought it was Lucifer, but then he noticed the eyes were not as powerful. He was face to face with a rattlesnake. Its tail was vibrating, its rattle sounding.

In his delirium, he wondered if the snake really existed, or if it was just a byproduct of his altered state of thinking. He watched the pit viper levitate away from him arching into strike mode. It seemed real. A snakebite was the last thing he needed. Sure it would bring his death quicker, which was the only thing he had to look forward to, but it might make the process that much more painful, which he was not looking forward to at all.

The snake was poised, but did not strike. Again, Abe questioned the reality of what he was seeing. If it was real, what was it waiting for?

He couldn't stand it any longer. He had to know if his predicament was real. Slowly, he reached out his hand knowing he would grasp empty air or get pierced by venom-dripping fangs.

As he reached out, the rattling intensified. The head of the snake retracted back almost to its tail. Abe stopped mid-reach. His tension was maxed. Everything froze. His hand, the snake; even the air around him felt still as if he existed within a hiccup of time. He didn't know what to do. His moisture-deprived brain was unable to make a decision.

Pop! The noise made him jump.

It sounded like a champagne bottle had popped right next to his ear. The snake was gone. Abe was confused. His eyes searched. He found the snake. It hadn't been a hallucination? He was still confused.

Inexplicably the reptile had slid a few feet away from him and was now writhing about in squirming coils of itself, headless.

Where did its head go? He wondered in a stupor. It was not normal for heads to simply disappear from snakes. That's when the shadow covered him. The buzzards were descending and that only meant one thing. He was dying.

He looked up at those who were coming for him. The shadows were wrong. They were too big and not at all buzzard-like.

Of all the shadows, he noticed one in particular. This shadow held a gun. "I told you I could blow its head off from there," the shadow spoke.

"Too bad we're not in Vegas," one of the other shadows said. "Because that was dang lucky."

The shadows laughed. Abe lost consciousness.

CHAPTER 65

Lucifer sat upon his throne, staring at Bob Gulam with eyes narrowed. He wasn't frustrated or angry with his number one human. He just enjoyed extracting fear from mortals.

Bob had been Lucifer's charge for a century. During that time, he had gifted Bob with physical immortality. It was easy for him to give out such gifts. After all, his power was no longer tethered as it had been.

He smiled because such gifts were never free. Physical immortality had been given in exchange for spiritual slavery. Lucifer's smile deepened because Bob's soul was as good as dead.

During the hundred years Lucifer had mentored Bob, Bob had never let him down, not once. In fact, Bob had become quite comfortable in his situation. Therefore, Lucifer conjectured, Bob should have no reason to fear him.

Still, he breathed in, hoping to catch the intoxicating scent he craved, even if it was only barely detectable. He exhaled and his inner smile faded. He was left wanting.

No matter. Bob Gulam's terror would soon be rekindled. Lucifer anticipated that day with longing. Once the gatekeeper was out of the way, he would send in troops. The siege of Geddon would begin and with its conclusion, with Geddon in ruins, his reign could begin in earnest. He could throw the charade of the Ra to the wind, and usher in his eternal reign of Hell on Earth. Those with the mark would finally understand what they had aligned with. But it would be too late. The door on that trap would have snapped shut, no escape.

Then the final step would occur. He would conquer God's Kingdom in heaven, as he had on earth. He would be unstoppable.

His inner smile returned as he thought of the inevitable future, and what he would do to God once God had been subdued. He would make him grovel at his feet, forever the dog under his table begging for scraps.

He took another drag on Bob's aura, but the fumes he inhaled remained free of fear. *No matter,* he thought. *In the long run, he will fear me and it will be well worth the wait.* He licked his lips in anticipation. *Patience, patience,* he thought. *Patience, after all is a virtue.*

Of course Lucifer was not a virtuous being. "Bob," he said.

"Yes, master," Bob answered.

"You have served me well. You have preached the way of the Ra without waiver."

"Yes, master."

"The only speck of filth left on this planet is Geddon."

"Do you want me to preach to them as well?"

Lucifer shook his head. "No. They will not heed our words. Those in Geddon are of the most stubborn breed."

Bob nodded.

"They are beyond help."

"What then are your orders concerning them?"

Lucifer liked Bob's enthusiasm. "There is only one thing left to do."

Bob nodded again with no emotion. The lack of feeling pleased Lucifer. Bob had always been loyal, even before he had known what he was loyal to. But these days, he was such a devotee that all others paled by comparison. "The final solution?" he asked hopefully.

"Spread the news," Lucifer said with a low, intimate tone. "We will march on Geddon."

Bob nodded, was dismissed and left Lucifer alone to savor the victory that would soon be his.

CHAPTER 66

Abe's soul was ablaze. The stench of fire and brimstone filled his nostrils. The smoke of Hell burned his eyes. He coughed violently, but the burning refused to diminish. He could hear the Ra laughing from inside him as they added fuel to the flames.

The fire that scorched his spirit sucked all the moisture from him. He was drying up like a salmon in a smokehouse. He wanted relief. He needed relief. There was none.

Just as things were becoming unbearable, coolness washed over him. The burning dryness continued, but the cooling on his forehead was like a miracle from heaven.

*

He awoke and opened his eyes. His nightmare was over—or was it? Some of what he had dreamt, he thought, was not a dream. It was reality. His esophagus still burned with dehydration. His flesh felt as dry as the long-dead parchment-skin of an Egyptian mummy.

He looked about, moving only his eyes, fearing that any more movement than that would cause him to disintegrate into dust and ash. His head ached, though he found relief in the cool, wet washcloth on his brow. Tendrils of cool water dripped down and around his ears. It was wonderful.

Tempting fate, but still hoping the whole dust and ash scenario would not come to fruition, he tried to sit up. He managed only to raise his head from the pillow, too weak to do more. His head pounded too much.

"Relax," came a voice.

A pair of hands reached from behind him and gently put his head back down upon the pillow. The hands were odd—too long and too white. In the corner, he saw the one who spoke. This was not the large-handed individual who stood behind him, out of his sight, but another.

"Relax," the man said again. Then he said something to the large-handed one. It sounded like gibberish to Abe; some sort of foreign tongue.

He angled his eyes up to see the owner of the hands. An involuntary gasp escaped his dry throat. Abe's mouth gaped; he could hear his own lips cracking under the pressure. The metallic taste of blood filled his mouth as it oozed from his bleeding lips. He barely registered the pain from the new injuries, in his amazement. The owner of the larger than life hands was himself, larger than life and unnaturally white—an albino basketball player. He looked into the eyes of this oddity. They were unreadable. The whole face was unreadable. The strange being could have been friendly or malicious. Abe hoped for the former, but the neutrality of the face gave no indication.

"Ah," the creature said breathily. Then he said more gibberish.

"My friend is glad to see you're awake," the man in the corner interpreted.

The language of this one was as bizarre as his appearance. The creature's movements were awkward largely due to the fact that the room was too small for his carriage. He had to slump over just to keep from bumping into the ceiling.

The white one lifted a nearby pitcher and poured a cup of water into a large tumbler. Abe found himself entranced by the way it moved, the way it walked; its very existence mesmerized him. It was both human and not, a paradox of sorts. It brought the water to Abe and, with one of its large hands, cradled Abe's head up from the pillow so he could drink. With its other hand, it held the cup to Abe's mouth.

The water tasted like blood, but that was his own doing. As he drank, the water became less bloody as the coldness of it cauterized his seeping lips and washed away the crimson flow. He didn't get as much down as he had hoped. Swallowing too hard, he choked and sprayed pink water onto his chest in foamy splotches of froth.

Just then, Abe became acutely aware that although he didn't have the mark of the Ra, he had come from them. He wondered if his origins were known to these who cared for him now. He had to explain.

He tried, but his lungs hurt too much and his head felt as if a railroad spike had been driven into it. His esophagus was gummy and held his words so they couldn't come out.

The one in the corner spoke. "Don't worry about anything now. Just rest today, for tomorrow will have worries of its own."

Abe didn't answer. Instead, he closed his eyes and drifted off. This time, the nightmare of the Ra did not return.

As deep sleep swallowed him, he swore he heard the man say "Welcome to Geddon." Then he was out.

CHAPTER 67

"And the smoke of their torment ascendeth up for ever and ever: and they have no rest day nor night." – Revelation 14:11.

*

JoAnne, like Bob, had been allowed to live all these years. However, in comparison, her existence had been her own personal Hell. She had not slept, not for a century. This would have been the death of her but that her possessor gave her energy.

It wasn't a wholesome energy, but akin to the sleeplessness that occurs from awaking out of a dreadful nightmare. But for her, there was no waking up. Her nightmare was perpetual.

One would think such anguish couldn't possibly last. Sooner or later, one would acclimate, desensitize, and grow numb to the pain. JoAnne wished for this. She begged for it, but was denied relief time and time again. The pain of possession only grew worse over the years. It cut her like a dull razor and the pain from those wounds only became more acute as her spiritual infection inflamed and grew.

Countless times she begged the demon within to let her go. Every time, the answer was the same. Splinter would laugh and wrench his grip on her just a little tighter.

The only thing that broke her from the constant punishment was her mundane duties. Tattoo after identical tattoo; she had been reduced to a Xerox machine. She did it because as long as she did her job, the demon within her dealt out lesser pain as a reward.

Men, women, and children came to her, received the mark from her hands, and lost their freedom. She looked every client in the eye, wishing she could warn them, but knowing such disclosure would not be tolerated by her host.

And there were the mighty bitey bugs. They haunted her day and night. Over the years, they became more powerful, more taunting, and more sadistic. They were invisible to all but her. She alone saw them. She alone was tortured by them. Such was the horror of the death in which she existed.

After a century of monotony, even the slightest change in schedule floored her. Such changes didn't occur often; almost never.

Today, she saw that a change was coming and she did not know what to make of it. She looked up from her work and saw something she had never before seen. She saw the end of the line. She only saw it for a moment before being forced back to task by her master, but she had seen it. She knew it was there.

She fretted with mixed feelings. On the one hand, she felt relief. She had begun to believe that her tattoo line would never end. Now that she saw otherwise, she relished the thought of a break. On the other hand, dread crept in. What would become of her now that her usefulness was no more? What more could they do to punish her?

She wondered and shuddered. Splinter knew her thoughts. He knew everything that went on within her. He provided no explanation, but chuckled—a malicious laugh, she'd grown to hate.

Over every inch of her flesh, she felt mighty bitey bugs slither and crawl. She knew this was only the pre-curser to what was yet to come. Vomit rose. She swallowed hard. Previous punishment had taught her Splinter did not appreciate vomiting slaves. She forced her bile back.

Splinter laughed louder. JoAnne lamented her predicament. The tattoos continued, at least for now.

CHAPTER 68

"And I heard the number of them which were sealed: and there were sealed an hundred and forty and four thousand." – Revelation 7:4.

*

Kerry listened to the old radio that sat on her kitchen table. Her heart sank. The Ra news network program had been interrupted by a special news bulletin, the anchor's voice replaced by none other than the King of Demons himself, giving a call to action, a call to war.

Those who were marked were ordered to assemble under the guidance of their regional leaders in preparation for an attack. The location of the future battle was given in longitude and latitude calculation. She knew those coordinates. The secret of Geddon was a secret no more.

In disgust Kerry turned off the broadcast. Her hands trembled. Her body felt unusually cold and clammy. Geddon, the town that had died only to be reborn, was now home to slightly more than 144,000 residents—quite impressive considering 50 years ago, it had been only herself and those in the graveyard.

The town was well provisioned. They had guns, ammunition, and food stored in mass quantities. But all of that was a drop in the bucket compared to what the marked ranks likely had. After all, Geddon was just a dot on the map, a small island of Christianity in a vast heathen ocean.

She thought back. Geddon had not always been so Christian. Before the arrival of Pastor Garrett, there was no church here. He came. He established the church. Geddon became a believing town. What a legacy that man left.

Back then, the town was just a speck, something easily overlooked, but those days were gone. The speck had become a mountain, and harder to miss.

She knew that whatever happened, God would give them what they needed. He had promised her through Scriptures that He would be with them, even to the close of the age.

That close now seemed just beyond the horizon. Thoughts of Matthew's description of the darkness chasing the Rogue flashed into her memory. Images of tsunamis of darkness flooded her mind. She saw the wave crashing down upon Geddon and gasped. With a prayer, she pushed to break the mental block of the lopsided odds. Geddon against the world. It seemed ludicrous. Hopeless.

With God all things are possible. She wasn't sure where the words came from, but she listened. She clung to them. It was all she had. God had placed her as the leader of Geddon for a purpose. As leader, she must set the example. They would all need to rely on the power of God, focusing on Him and remembering God takes care of his children even in the darkest of places.

She turned the radio back on. Despite her newly-found strength, what she heard made her skin crawl. It was a live speech, reminiscent of old Nazi propaganda broadcasts; and the words reminiscent of Hitler himself.

Lucifer was preaching an unholy liturgy. He shouted over the airwaves, "Arms to Geddon!" and the crowd responded in kind.

Lucifer shrieked again, "Arms to Geddon!"

The crowd answered again.

"Arms to Geddon!"

The multitudes roared back, only partially intelligible with the thousands of voices shouting at once.

The sound shook Kerry to the core. It was not *Arms to Geddon* she heard, but *Armageddon!* The crowd chanted over and over and over. Kerry staggered and fell backwards, falling in a chair.

"Armageddon! Armageddon! *Armageddon!*"

*

"If any man worship the beast and his image, and receive his mark in the forehead, or in his hand. The same shall drink the wine of the wrath of God." – Revelation 14:9-10.

*

Lucifer gave the signal and the live feed was cut. Wordlessly, he commanded his demon-army. He smiled. It was a command he had been waiting to give for a very, very long time. The moment had arrived.

Go forth and possess all with the mark, he ordered.

His legions obeyed.

Lucifer had to sit down, relishing the moment. In an instant, the world came to know who the Ra truly was. In that instant, the world shrieked in terror, a tidal wave of terror that smashed into him with tsunami force. He soaked it in, his face lifted to the skies, laughing. The high was exquisite, absolutely exquisite. The dizziness of ecstasy overwhelmed him.

For those with the mark, the shock was immense. It was the moment a rabbit scurries into a hole only to discover a cobra waiting. Lucifer sensed the shock. He loved it, drinking it in like fine wine.

CHAPTER 69

A commotion jolted Abe awake. He had no idea how long he had been out, but by the ache in his muscles and the stiffness in his joints, he suspected it had been a while. He touched his lips and winced. They were tender; dry and crusty. At least they were no longer bleeding.

He sat up slowly, letting the dizziness settle before swinging his legs over the side of the bed, testing them cautiously. They looked as spindly as a spider's. He had lost quite a bit of body mass in his confinement. Once confident they would support him, he took a few tentative steps.

The commotion that had aroused him continued. The uproar was just outside his window. He looked around. He was alone in the room. The tall one who had nursed him was nowhere to be found. He wondered if it had been a hallucination.

He approached the window, drawn by the commotion outside. Through the closed curtains, he spied shadows. He edged them apart. At the sight outside, his weak legs nearly gave way.

A group had gathered, some wearing white robes. These were being led by a woman—an ancient stooped woman with long white hair held into a ponytail by a black ribbon. She looked as weak as he felt. Her hand trembled on a cane as she put her weight upon it and that tremble reverberated throughout her whole elderly frame.

She turned and for a moment, Abe swore she looked right at him with unnaturally brown eyes, the color of rich dark chocolate, so deep they were almost black. His mind flashed to the room with the drain and the dead bodies. The prophet had ordered him to murder this woman. The thought sickened him.

She led the robed ones to a trough not twenty feet outside his room, which she climbed into. Her dress grew wet and clingy as water flowed over the brim and onto the hardened clay of the earth.

The white-robed people lined up beside the trough and for an instant everything seemed to pause, a moment in time. In that moment, Abe found he wanted one of the white robes for himself.

The woman motioned to one of them, who entered the trough with her. She murmured something Abe couldn't make out. Once again, everything seemed to stall briefly before lurching back to life. She laid the robed one back into the water completely submerging him below the surface. Abe was surprised at her strength. How was she capable of immersing a full-grown man? She plucked him back up out of the water just as effortlessly. With hands raised and a broad grin, he exited the trough. The next in line entered. The process was repeated until all of the white-robed ones had been dunked.

Witnessing the joy on the faces of those who exited the trough made Abe want to wear one of their white robes all the more. He didn't understand why or what was so great about this woman's dunking, but he wanted in.

He was about to leave the window and go out to see if he could be dunked, when everything changed. The happy people grew wary. The old woman frowned. Her brown eyes narrowed. Her hands clenched into fists, the one with the cane in a white-knuckled grip. At the same time, her tremors increased. The sky turned black and a crack of lightning split the sky.

Abe's heart began to race.

The lightning crashed again and when the brilliance faded, a great beast stood before the trough. About its massive head flailed many other heads, skinny, eyeless, and sharp like needles. It had a gaping wound in its chest, though the wound seemed healed.

Abe drew back. It was the beast that had feasted on those with him in the room with the drain. It spoke. Despite the glass between them, Abe heard every blasphemous word. "I curse you who are blessed!" It roared, shaking its head. "I curse you who are baptized in the name of the lamb who was slain!"

Abe's mind told him to run away and hide. Terror held him tight. Unable to move, he watched the horror unfold. The beast circled the robed ones, herding them into a tight little bunch, blaspheming and salivating. Yet it didn't attack. Abe leaned forward, watching. A beast like that should have no problem tearing these unarmed ones to pieces.

Then it hit him. It *couldn't* attack. Because of whose baptism they had received, the beast had no power to harm them. His heart sank. He had not been baptized. He was not under that protection.

As the realization struck him, the beast turned. It peered through his window, into his gaze. It licked its evil chops and smiled. One of the pointy eyeless heads rose to strike and Abe knew he didn't stand a chance. He closed his eyes, a shield against coming death. He heard his own voice scream as something hit him. Then he felt nothing.

Still, he screamed and writhed, fighting the evil thing with all he had. Slowly, he realized nothing more was striking him.

He didn't want to see the beast, but he had to know where it was. He opened his eyes. It was gone! That which he wrestled was a blanket.

Could it have all just been a nightmare? He looked around. He had fallen from the bed. His cloths were soaked and acrid with sweat. His hair was matted and damp.

He climbed up off the floor and went to the window. Sunlight stabbed through the drawn curtains, illuminating the fabric in a most inviting way. He approached the window, cautiously parting the curtains, and looked out.

CHAPTER 70

Lucifer was happier than he'd been in centuries—if ever. The report had reached him. All of those with the mark had been possessed. The charade could stop. The disguises had been shed. All with the mark knew their leader: Lucifer, King of Demons, Lord of Hell, master of all and servant to none.

He felt the suffering of the possessed around the world. *Exquisite!* He felt their shock at discovering they'd been duped. He tasted their terror at realizing who they had committed their loyalty to and whose mark they had received.

He laughed, head thrown back in glee, as he thought of the mighty bitey bugs that had harassed JoAnne all these years. Now they harassed all the slaves. Their pain, their cries and shouts, rose up as a fragrant offering to him. It was a wonderful odor.

There was one he had set aside, at least for now. He liked Bob Gulam. That, however was not the reason he reserved from him the damnation due. No, he still had a use for Bob.

"You called for me?"

Lucifer turned, seeing the only Marked One who still believed the lies. "Yes Bob, I called for you."

"I came as quickly as I could."

Lucifer's grin took on a sadistic tinge. "I know you did, Bob. You've always been so eager to please me. Rest assured, such loyalty has not gone unnoticed."

"I have alerted everyone worldwide via the media. They are all playing the recording you requested. We will march on Geddon!" Bob's statement bore conviction.

Lucifer nodded. "Well done, my good and faithful servant. You will go with me into battle at my side."

"To destroy those without the mark?"

Lucifer chuckled. "Perhaps, I'm not sure."

"But you said their time to join us was over."

Lucifer breathed in Bob's frustration, laced with murderous rage. He enjoyed it immensely. He could always count on Bob for a good old-fashioned buzz. This time would be no exception. Bob wanted more than to simply kill the unmarked. He wanted to wipe them from existence in the most diabolical way possible.

By reneging on his previous promise, Lucifer knew he would create the cocktail he craved from Bob. He breathed in more of Bob's feelings and held it in as long as possible, to savor every ounce. He exhaled slowly. "You're not happy with that answer?"

Bob said nothing, but the intoxicants from him verified he was not.

"Be honest, my servant." Lucifer dropped just a hint of authority into the statement.

"I was just wondering why these people deserve to go on living."

Deception was one of Lucifer's best talents. "Isn't it right to show mercy if possible? I would like you to be there with me, my trusted prophet. I would like you to preach the truth to them one more time, to see if any of these most stubborn mules will believe."

"They're all idiots!" Bob retorted, forgetting whom he addressed. "They've gone to great lengths to not accept the truth. Why would they accept it now?"

Lucifer nodded.

"They've suffered discrimination and beatings. They've lost their jobs and homes. We made their lives miserable." Bob glared. "They are a stiff-necked remnant of the old order."

"So you feel it is a lost cause?" Lucifer asked.

Bob didn't answer and Lucifer guessed why. No answer would be correct. If he said it was not a lost cause, he would have lost the debate. To say otherwise would be to contradict his boss. His only answer was the trembling of his body as Bob saw the trap.

Lucifer absorbed those trembles. *What a rush!* He could always count on good old Bob for a fun time.

"You will go with me to Geddon. You will try your best to persuade this last remnant."

"Yes, Master," Bob said through gritted teeth.

The bitterness that oozed from Bob to Lucifer was the perfect garnish to a perfect cocktail. He took it in and cherished every last drop.

CHAPTER 71

Kerry sat in silence in the dark room that matched her mood. This had been her state since first hearing of the impending invasion of Geddon. She prayed continuously. Still, it seemed inevitable. Geddon was doomed.

She'd always suspected this day would come. A secret like Geddon couldn't remain hidden indefinitely, especially with its metamorphosis from ghost town to metropolis.

She sighed deeply and forced herself to think of all the blessings God had bestowed. Truly God had provided. Truly God was good. Geddon should not exist at all in its present state. Too many people had come. The well should have dried up. The crops which grew in fields for miles around the city should have died in the desert heat. The game in the area should be non-existent instead of abundant.

The well had not depleted. The crops had not died, the game had not gone extinct. That Geddon thrived was a miracle unto itself. Indeed, they had been blessed. Until now. Geddon had been discovered by the enemy. The countdown to the final battle had begun.

She prayed earnestly in the words of her savior when He had prayed in the garden of Gethsemane. She prayed this cup might pass from her. She had more to pray in order to finish out the prayer that Jesus had prayed so long ago, but the words were difficult to spit out. Finally, her head hanging, she whispered, "Not my will, but yours be done."

The words knotted her stomach. It frightened her because it took herself out of the equation. The prayer was no longer the demand her sinful self wanted it to be. No, it was a request, and a disclaimer: God should do what He felt was best.

Tears slid down her wrinkled cheeks. She knew it was in God's hands. She was never more than a servant. Still, she could not help but wish her will upon the Almighty.

Strangely, though, slowly, her mind cleared and her body relaxed. A voice spoke, not audibly but internally. "I am with you always, even to the very end of the age." She knew who spoke. These were the words of Jesus Christ. This was his promise to all who clung to Him.

Whatever the future held, even if it was defeat by a seemingly overwhelming enemy, her savior would be there with her. This was the message she would take to the people of Geddon.

A knock at her door jarred her. She rose, opening the door to her friend, the young man from Outer Earth.

"Sorry to disturb you," he said awkwardly.

She smiled. "It's quite okay, Moses. What is it?"

Moses didn't return her smile, but that meant nothing. He rarely smiled. She couldn't blame him what with all of his losses. "The new arrival," Moses said. "He is..um...agitated."

"How so?"

"He wants to be baptized."

Kerry nodded. "Where is he?"

Moses pointed the way and Kerry headed off with her walking cane in hand. If it was a baptism that was needed, then it was a baptism she would do.

*

Abe stood outside the house in which he had been recovering. He had left quickly, on looking out that window and seeing a trough was there just as it had been in his dream. He didn't know what it all meant. All he knew was he wanted protection from the beast. If that vision was to be believed, he needed to do as the beast from his vision had said. He needed to be baptized—in the name of the lamb who was slain!

He hadn't realized until that moment how distant he had grown from the Ra. Their generosity, if it could be called that, now paled. Yes, they'd offered him a life free of discrimination, but then, they were the ones who had discriminated against him in the first place. In contrast, the people of Geddon had taken him in. They'd found him in the desert and shown true love in nursing him back to health. After such acts of kindness, how could he obey the Ra? How could he kill their leader? The answer was simple. He could not.

*

Kerry found him staggering about in the street in front of the house in which they had been keeping him. She heard him begging all who passed by. He wanted to be baptized into the name of the lamb who was slain.

She chuckled inside. This was quite exciting. He turned to her. Their eyes locked. He went silent.

*

Abe was in shock. Before him stood the one with the deep brown eyes. He took a step towards her and found his voice. "You are to baptize me in the name of the lamb who was slain. Whatever that means."

She shook her head. "I cannot."

"Why not?" he demanded. "I have to!"

"First," she said, "you must *believe* in the lamb who was slain. Through Him your salvation lies. Without that, your baptism will be meaningless."

"I want to believe," Abe declared.

"That's a start."

"Please...teach me."

She smiled and a tear trickled out from one of her eyes. "Let's start with the Gospel." She led him back toward the house, telling him the good news.

He listened. He believed.

CHAPTER 72

Rage lashed through Lucifer's heart! He *felt* his assassin's loyalty trickle away from him. He had defected.

Lucifer felt it in his bones! He had underestimated the power of kindness and love which the enemy was so adept at displaying. This was a trait he lacked. So, in playing to his strengths, he would show the opposite. He would retaliate with unbridled fury and hatred. He shot up off his throne. "Bob!"

Bob cowered before him. "Yes, Lord Lucifer."

"Our assassin has failed! The leader will not be as dead as we hoped, when we converge upon Geddon."

Bob said nothing. He didn't know what to say.

"This will make your job more difficult. With their leader in place, you will have to try even harder to persuade them to commit to the receiving of their marks."

"Why not simply wipe them off the face of the earth?" Bob objected.

Lucifer rubbed his temples. Bob, despite his loyalty, could be a burden. "I want them to have one last chance to join us!" His eyes blazed at Bob. "I want to show a final gesture of mercy."

In truth, he was no more able to extend mercy than he was able to show kindness, but Bob didn't need to know that. Lucifer didn't wish to explain the wound he dealt to the triune God every time a soul was branded with the marks of Hell. He couldn't very well tell him that, without divulging that the Ra were not who they claimed to be.

He didn't want Bob to know this yet. He needed him committed to the cause—a wholehearted prophet to witness to the souls of Geddon.

Bob didn't answer, but bowed in submission. Lucifer put his hand on Bob's bowed head. He felt his slave shiver at the contact. That Bob squirmed improved Lucifer's mood significantly. He even managed something akin to a grin. Lucifer fed off his fear, cherished it!

CHAPTER 73

Abe was lifted from the water, born again. He hadn't been sure what to expect, or what would happen next. Kerry wrapped him in a warm hug. "Welcome to the fold," she said as those who had gathered cheered. A few of those closest slapped him on the back.

A load had been lifted. Everything felt brighter. Everything felt clearer. For the first time in his life, he didn't feel the pressure of the Ra or the temptation to follow them. He felt free! He knew he was with the people to whom he belonged. He had been born again. Baptized in the name of the lamb who was slain.

He knew Jesus. He knew the true identity of the Ra. It was an identity he had always suspected but never confirmed. He would never follow the enemy again, but would hold onto his new savior.

One of the witnesses to his baptism was the one who had nursed him back to health. Indeed, this one's size had not been a hallucination. He was ten feet tall and as skinny as a beanpole. Stepping from the trough, Abe went to him. "Thanks for everything."

The expressionless pale face of the tall one looked down at him. The giant said nothing, but silently extended its hand.

Abe took it. "I owe you my life."

"You owe him nothing." Abe turned and saw the one who had acted as interpreter previously. He now knew him by name: Moses. "There are no debts here. You would have done the same for us."

Abe dropped his eyes. He had been sent to kill Kerry. He felt the need to confess. He opened his mouth.

The brown-eyed woman interrupted. "Whatever you were before today—that is an old life, a dead life. You are a new creation, given the opportunity to start over. Whatever wrongs you did in that life are forgotten. Whatever wrongs you do from this point on will be forgiven through belief that the lamb who was slain can wash away all sins through repentance."

Abe closed his mouth. Suddenly, it seemed inappropriate to explain himself. He was happy as he stood there at the dawn of a new life. He was blameless. He was home.

CHAPTER 74

Bob Gulam was confused. For the first time, in a century, the Ra were strangely absent. Not one could be found except Lucifer who seemed perpetually present.

Bob had asked his master why the Ra had abandoned them just as the great siege of Geddon was about to begin. Lucifer had answered curtly with a question of his own. "The approaching battle is the Earth's. Do you really think the Marked Ones cannot defeat this small pocket of the unmarked without the Ra?"

There was only one answer Bob could give, only one answer expected of him. He shook his head.

"There may be no need for battle at all," Lucifer said smoothly, "if you are persuasive."

Bob imagined the siege of Geddon. It would be a great moment for mankind as the whole world converged on the few too stubborn to accept evolution and become something greater than human.

And therein lay the rub. Bob didn't want any Geddonites to join their ranks. Why should they be allowed to save their skins now? *Now*, after being a thorn in his side for so long? *They didn't deserve it!*

Lucifer brought Bob from his thoughts. "In three days, we march on Geddon."

*

What an idiot!

Lucifer had ordered Bob to do another redundant task. Frankly, he had grown tired of the imp always hanging around him, as if Bob was worthy of being always in his presence. He tolerated him, for the sake of that one final task. Even though the assassin had failed to kill the Gatekeeper, Lucifer was sure many from Geddon would come to them after hearing Bob's final speech.

He knew Bob didn't like allowing these late-comers into the fold. But poor gullible Bob *still* hadn't figured out this was all much deeper than alliances with benevolent inter-dimensional travelers. Lucifer wanted to get as many to abandon the enemy as possible. He didn't care if it happened a century ago, now, or at the last possible moment. By pulling people away from God, he weakened Him. And the weaker his enemy, the better.

Telepathically, he reached out to his minions who possessed those with the mark. *In three days, we march on Geddon.* His time frame would not go unnoticed by the enemy. Just as the Christ took three days to descend into his realm to announce that battle's victory, so now he would take three days to win the last battle and therefore...the war.

He rubbed his hands with anticipation. Untethered power was truly his. His reign would soon begin.

*

Aganju cranked the pressure tighter; tighter and tighter until the breaking point. The one he possessed cried out, begging for mercy.

Such pleas brought joy to this demon. It brought joy, but not mercy.

He wrenched the already-twisted soul in his gnarled demonic hands, feeling the pain wring from it. It was a most lovely experience.

Aganju's charge now knew the truth. The truth most certainly did not set him free. Indeed, it was too late for this poor soul to escape the slavery into which he had been chained.

Still, he disallowed the prisoner from telling Bob Gulam what was really going on behind the stage-curtains. In fact, Bob had become something of a cosmic joke—the only one who still believed the lies of the Ra.

Aganju felt the prisoner squirm as Bob approached, informing them the final battle would begin in three days. Aganju and his slave already knew. But Lucifer had sent Bob on this errand to inform as many as possible. Aganju could see why his master needed a break from the one foolish human who still believed in the Ra. He was so *clingy*, and so proud of his position.

Of course it was for convenience Lucifer had given this mortal such a position and it was a position he would soon be stripped of. Aganju smiled and nodded through the one he possessed as Bob informed.

Bob left, looking for more to tell, loyal to the end. Aganju shook his head and chuckled. The lie continued for the one last mortal still drinking the Kool-Aid. Soon, though, the thin-plaster wall of lies would crumble and even Bob—foolish Bob—would see the truth behind it. Aganju anticipated that moment. It would be glorious and he hoped he would be present when it all went down. Bob would go into a full-panic mode. The fumes wafting from him would be rare and gourmet. In his joy, he tormented his captive. The captive shrieked in pain. Aganju laughed.

CHAPTER 75

Kerry needed help getting to the podium. The stage was too high. Her legs were too old, her muscles too weak. Moses helped her on one side. Her cane help on the other. The future of Geddon hung in the balance. She didn't feel like a leader, but that was what she had become. Age slowed her approach.

She looked at Moses. Eighty years her junior, there was no way they were siblings. Yet, she felt an odd connection to this man. It was beyond her understanding, yet she could not deny how she felt towards this man who had come to her through a door from another dimension. Finally, they reached the podium. She tapped her finger on the microphone to make sure it was live.

A stage-hand gave Moses a microphone as well. Kerry knew she would need to speak slowly and clearly with many pauses. Moses would interpret for the tall white ones.

She thought about Moses, this strange enigma of a man who belonged everywhere and nowhere at the same time. He had told her his story and the story of his parents. He was from Inner Earth, but had been born in Outer Earth. He had been raised there, but had never really fit in there. His size and emotions didn't match up. He had two homes—yet he was homeless.

She glanced at him. He nodded. It was go time. She began what was likely to be her last speech to the citizens of Geddon. She spoke.

*

Hello, citizens of Geddon. I'm not good at speeches. I don't know why God made me leader, but he has and I will not question it. I have only this to say.

She looked out over the crowd, filling the square, the streets beyond, past her view, and spoke into the microphone. *You have all heard the broadcasts and know our city is no longer as hidden as we had hoped. In three days, they will converge upon our town.*

What will they do to us? I don't have any answer.

So what can we do? We will do as we have always done. We will put our faith in Christ. We will stand firm on that solid foundation and will not be swayed no matter what the enemy threatens or what they may do.

Remember the words from Matthew's gospel. Do not fear those who kill the body but cannot kill the soul. Rather fear him who can destroy both soul and body in Hell.

The bottom line is this. If we die, we are destined for paradise as our faith promises. If we live, the enemy will have no hold on us, again because of our faith.

She waited for Moses to translate. With his last words uttered, an intense silence filled the space. In that silence, she left the podium. Moses set aside his microphone and helped her back down the stairs. They walked through the crowd, arm in arm, people parting before them.

Her head drooped. She was no leader. She feared she did no good with her speech. Still, she had done the best she could. The chant from the enemy's broadcast echoed over and over in her mind as she moved through the Geddonite crowd. It was not *arms to Geddon* as was supposed, but *Armageddon.*

She recalled the days before the great migration, back when she was the sole inhabitant of Geddon California. She had been so lonely, but God had cured her loneliness. He had cured it 144,000 times over.

Now, as she passed through the crowd, she found herself wishing those days of solitude would return. She had not asked to be a leader of so many. She had not asked for this. Her thoughts spiraled downward as she continued through the masses. She chastised herself. Everything was in God's plan; her inner-tantrum was like slapping her creator in the face. Who was she after all? Nothing but a vapor in the wind, here today and gone tomorrow. How dare she, being what she was, question God?

She was nothing compared to God. Yet God had loved her so much he had sent his son Jesus to die and rise from the dead to make her worthy of salvation. All of the citizens of Geddon fell into that category—all doomed if judged on their own sinful souls. It was only their faith in Jesus that saved them. It was only through Jesus that their sins had been erased.

The downward spiral reversed as these thoughts permeated her mind. They had gathered in Geddon as a united group of Christians; God would not abandon them, not now when they needed him most. As she continued through the crowd, she began to sing a hymn.

Those around her joined in. Soon, a thunderous chorus resounded in the desert and she was reminded of the words from the book of Isaiah in the Bible of John the Baptist, the voice of one calling in the desert. *In the wilderness, prepare the way for the Lord; make straight in the desert a highway for our God.*

Indeed she would make sure the path was straight. Her spirit improved with every step she took.

CHAPTER 76

Lucifer smiled as the sun rose above the horizon. It was the beginning of the third day: a day scheduled for destruction! He could hardly wait. Every human being with the mark and every demonic host within those damned souls were on the move. Soon, they would converge upon the little spot of desert on which the last battle would commence.

A hundred years ago, such a mass migration would have been impossible in such a short period of time. Now, under the guise of technology bestowed to mankind by the benevolent Ra, what had been impossible had become quite possible. It was, in truth, untethered demonic power. But the lie of technology had kept men working on the equipment: ultra-sonic trains that traveled over a thousand miles per hour; transports that flew many times faster than sound; hovercrafts like giant cattle cars capable of moving thousands at a time.

Lucifer's grin widened. Mankind was treading into unknown territory. It was ground they no doubt wished they were not treading, now they knew the truth, now they knew they were but slaves to demons. Lucifer chuckled as he thought of the one human being still in the dark. Poor gullible Bob! The fool!

Of course, even he would know the truth soon enough. Lucifer paced back and forth in the palace that years ago had been a humble cult compound but had since grown into a mighty fortress. Suddenly he lifted his head and shouted, "Bob!"

Bob came trembling into the room. Lucifer smiled. Bob always hovered within hearing range, unless on an assignment.

Bob bowed low. "Yes, Master?"

"The time has come."

Bob nodded.

"Today, the inhabitants of Geddon will convert or die!"

Bob nodded again.

"Today will be a historic day to be remembered always."

"Yes," Bob hissed.

"Say it louder!" Lucifer growled. "Be proud of what you have done, my good and faithful servant!"

"*Yes*!" Bob screamed.

"That's better." Lucifer's smile returned. "Be proud. It is all because of you this has occurred."

"Yes!" Bob shrieked again. His face grew red with fervor. His eyes glittered.

Satan's smile grew. It was another lie. Bob hadn't made things happen any more than an ax made a tree fall without a lumberjack to wield it. But it never hurt to instill feelings of loyalty. In addition, if Bob, somehow, got wind of the truth before Lucifer wished, it would be in his favor that Bob felt responsible for summoning all the demons of Hell. Guilt was a powerful tool.

A sly look invaded Lucifer's face as he regarded Bob. "Today, the battle lines will be drawn. Today, you will be with me at my side."

Bob did not shout this time, but simply nodded.

*

Bob had such a mixture of feelings—almost too many to control. He couldn't believe, after such a long wait, that the goal had almost been reached. Pride flushed him—he had brought it all about, this new world! He had done that!

Yet he was also frustrated that he had to give the people of Geddon one more chance to turn to the rightful leaders of the world. He didn't want any of them joining the Union of the Ra. They had waited too long—a century! *A century!* They were lucky Lucifer was so merciful. If it had been up to him, no mercy would be given.

He was worried that he didn't know what this meant, long-term. His early life had been filled with the search for truth. Then the truth had arrived, giving him the responsibility to preach the Ra to the masses. That responsibility was now complete. So after today, what would be his purpose?

The answer to this question eluded him. He must bank on history, he decided. The Ra had been faithful to him, keeping their promises and giving him a high place of authority. His future with them would certainly be bright.

Such was his hope. It felt weak, but it was all he had to cling to so he dug his nails in and clung.

CHAPTER 77

Kerry stood, Moses on one side and Abe the other, watching the third day dawn.

The moment was filled with intense, unnatural quiet that screamed over the desert; a silent scream. She glanced at Moses. It was strange how this young man, so recently come into her life from another earth, shared with her a deep connection, a kinship. He had told her his story, of how he had come to be without his father and mother, of the destruction of Outer Earth. She shuddered. It appeared Inner Earth was about to follow suit. *I am with you always, even to the very close of the age.* Those words were barely present that morning. She hoped he felt stronger than she. His expression didn't give her confidence.

She turned to Abe. Of course he was there. He was always nearby, always reading the Bible he'd been given, always asking questions as new believers often do. Abe was unlike the others of Geddon because he had been with the Ra. She suspected he didn't know she knew. He didn't bear the mark of the enemy, but she saw the fear in his eyes, a dread only seen in those who had been with the enemy; a hopeless, fearful, dread. It had started to fade with his baptism. Even now, just days since his rebirth, it was almost gone. He was growing in his faith and understanding. She was hopeful that with time, that look of dread would leave him altogether.

Her focus returned to the rising sun. She wondered what the day would bring. She was sure she already knew. Yet, despite the pending apocalypse, joy filled her. Living or dying didn't matter. All that mattered was keeping the faith and encouraging the others of Geddon to do the same.

*

He'd never met anyone like Kerry, Abe thought, and suspected he never would again. He could see why God had chosen her to lead the city. She had helped him in so many ways. For the first time in his life he had true hope in his heart. Sure, he had been hopeful when he decided to go to the Ra and receive the mark, but being hopeful and having true hope, he'd found, were two different things. He had thanked her repeatedly until she told him to stop, saying she was just a fellow human on the same path as he, and nothing special.

Of course to him, she was something special. She was the one who had opened his eyes to the true savior and baptized him—a baptism that was just the beginning. Every minute that passed strengthened his faith. Every minute that ticked by weakened the Ra's hold on him—or rather the demons'. It made him sick to think he had actually contemplated assassinating this woman. It was a crime that, thankfully, he would never commit.

He wanted to tell her about his past, about his mission, but every time he began to confess, she interrupted, telling him whatever he had done was forgotten by God through repentance and no longer existed.

Still, he felt the need to confess. He had confessed to God, but someday, he would tell Kerry. For now he would be content in God's forgiveness, a mercy he couldn't understand but accepted, and was grateful for.

He watched the new day, the last day, break over the eastern horizon, and prayed for strength. He would need it. He was about to face his old masters. They would not be merciful.

I will be with you even to the very end of the age. The words came to him as he prayed, as he watched the sun rise. He drew strength from the promise. What a strange sensation. He felt balanced on the precipice of a new age. Despite his prayers, he felt a weakness in his bones. He pushed the doubt from him as best he could, but it lingered like a specter from his past, haunting him. His knees quivered.

CHAPTER 78

"And the number of the army of the horsemen were two hundred thousand thousand. And thus I saw the horses in the vision, and them that sat on them, having breastplates of fire, and jacinth, and brimstone: and the heads of the horses were as the heads of lions; and out of their mouths issued fire and smoke and brimstone." – Revelation 9:16-17.

*

Bob Gulam sat beside Lucifer on the small hover-craft as they drew nearer to Geddon. Despite the twinge of fear he always felt, so close to his master, things were pretty good for Bob. They traveled south from what he still nostalgically referred to as the Union of Seekers compound but in reality had become so much more. He looked out the window as they cruised a hundred feet above the surface. What he saw took his breath away.

As far as the eye could see flowed a sea of flesh, thousands upon thousands all obeying orders, all marching towards a single target. The glory of the army of the Ra was beyond words.

The troops, in matching uniforms, rode strange horse-like creatures. Bob turned to ask Lucifer where the creatures had come from and how everyone had been provisioned so quickly with the uniforms, but Lucifer in his usual way seemed to know Bob's thoughts. He answered before the question was uttered.

"The creatures are from my homeland. They are a sturdy breed. The uniforms were a last minute touch. I think it shows solidarity don't you?"

Bob closed his mouth and nodded. Looking out the window once again, he thought 'solidarity' didn't even begin to describe what he felt as he looked upon the vast army that covered the ground like an all-consuming invasion of locusts. The steeds' bestial heads gave them predatory looks, like lions. Their tails reminded him of eyeless snakes.

The strangest thing about these forces was their smell; sulfur, fire and brimstone. Indeed, they seemed to be covered in what could only be described as flames—but flames that didn't burn them up. It reminded him of the ancient story of Moses and the burning bush. He wondered if that fairy tale was just another incident of ancient man misinterpreting the signs of the Ra.

No! He shook his head. Even today, such ignorance persisted, the people of Geddon clinging to their useless superstitions. He looked over the force that would soon overwhelm the last bastion of ignorance. A smile grew on his face. It would be a great day indeed.

The hovercraft flew above and beyond the invasion, leaving the front line behind. "We must reach Geddon first," Lucifer announced matter-of-factly.

It made Bob nervous. He preferred the safety of numbers. He didn't care to be alone at the front, facing an enemy surely armed for battle. Sure, he hadn't aged for a century, but he didn't know if that made him immortal. He assumed bullets could still kill him. Even by Lucifer's side, he felt vulnerable.

Again, Lucifer seemed to know Bob's worries. "Don't concern yourself. It's simply a matter of diplomacy. I want you there first to prophecy to those in Geddon. I want to come to them before the threat arrives so they have an opportunity to join us not by coercion, but by their own free will."

"And if they won't?"

Lucifer simply smiled.

That was answer enough for Bob. He returned the smile. His nervousness evaporated. It was going to be a glorious day.

*

They traveled on. Bob had stopped looking out the hovercraft's window, preferring to go over his plan for preaching to the idiots of Geddon. These were the most stubborn of the stubborn and he doubted many would convert. Still, he found solace in knowing those which remained would have to confront the army he had seen. Geddon didn't stand a chance.

"Behold, the land of Geddon!" Lucifer disrupted Bob's thought.

Bob looked out the hovercraft's window and saw something unexpected. "I thought Geddon was in the desert?"

"It is."

Bob stared out at fields and vineyards. It didn't appear to be a desert.

"Deserts can be deceiving, Bob. No doubt there is some sort of aquafer beneath the surface the people have tapped into."

Bob huffed. "They probably think the water is a gift from their God."

Lucifer nodded. "That's true. I'm glad you're here to witness to them. They must be persuaded to believe in the Ra. Only then can I take them under my wing."

There was something odd about the fields and vineyards. Until that moment, Bob couldn't figure out what it was. Now it hit him. "Where is everyone? Where are those who tend the fields?"

Lucifer chuckled. "Our coming is no surprise to them, of this I am certain. They're waiting for us in their city."

Bob nodded.

"Being all together, they feel strength in their numbers, but that will actually play to our favor. You'll be able to witness to them all at once."

Bob nodded again. In the distance, a skyline appeared. This was his first glimpse of Geddon, California.

CHAPTER 79

The sun had risen half-way to high noon when the rushing noise became audible in Kerry's ears. She didn't know what the sound meant. She glanced at Moses. By his dumbfounded expression, she guessed he was in the dark with her. Abe, however, obviously recognized it. His expression did not put her mind at ease.

"What is it?" she asked, as Abe took a step back.

"It's a hovercraft's engine. The enemy approaches." His voice wavered as he spoke.

She looked in the direction from whence the noise came and spied a small black speck on the distant horizon. It grew steadily larger with every second until it was not a speck at all, but a massive flying machine. It hovered like a dragonfly, but far more sinister. "Do not fear them," she said with resolution. Deep down though, she felt less resolved.

*

She doesn't understand, Abe thought. *I was one of them, their assigned assassin; the one who failed his assignment. Now, they'll know I'm a defector.* Tears formed as he thought of the terrible things in store for him. Images of a door without a knob on one side and a drain in the floor flooded his memories. Flashbacks hit him, as solid as flying bricks, of dead bodies and eyeless snakes. Lucifer himself permeated his brain. A whimper escaped his lips.

He took another step back, but Moses put his arm around him. "There's no need to fear them. We are of the light. We are children of the lamb who was slain, who has promised to be with us until the end of the age. He is our protector if you only keep your faith."

"But you don't know the truth," Abe hissed. "None of you know the truth!" He pulled free.

"We know what they are," Kerry said. "They are demons."

"But you don't know what they're capable of."

"We know more than you think," Kerry said calmly.

"No, you don't! If you did, you never would have let me live! You would have let me die in the desert where you found me."

"You were with the Ra," Kerry said. "This I know. I don't know why they sent you here, but I can guess it was to harm us."

Abe blinked in surprise before retorting. "If you knew that much, why did you allow me live?"

Kerry smiled. "Because God is love."

Her words overwhelmed Abe.

She continued. "Even if we possessed ten times the power of our enemies, we would be nothing without love."

"No," Abe started to say, but she spoke.

"That's one of the flaws of the enemy. They are incapable of love. That's why they can't stand us—and that we follow the true God. They're not of the light. They cannot be saved as we are."

"Saved?" Abe gasped. "They outnumber us thousands to one. They're coming for us. We can't be saved!"

"They're just demons," Moses piped in. "By now, you must see that. They murdered my entire world. Trust me, I know what they're capable of." Moses' voice contained a bitterness that would make the cheapest coffee taste as sweet as sugar.

Abe looked wildly at them both. He wasn't sure how to make them understand, but they'd shown such kindness to him, he needed to help them live if he could. He needed to convince them to beg the enemy for mercy.

"Abe," Kerry's voice was gentle but firm. "Why did you feel so compelled to be baptized?"

He said nothing. Time seemed to freeze momentarily.

"Why?" she repeated.

He looked into her deep eyes as he recalled. "Because of my vision."

She nodded. "Tell us of your vision."

"I needed to be baptized to receive protection."

"Protection from what?"

He didn't answer. He knew where this conversation was going and it wasn't supportive of his current stand. The sound of the hovercraft was now deafening and kicking up the dust of the desert. "Protection from them!" He finally screamed pointing at the hovercraft above.

"So why are you so afraid now? You received that baptism. You accepted that Jesus changed you. He promised to be with you to the end. Jesus *will* protect you."

Abe opened his mouth, but no response came. He felt torn between two insane options—beg for mercy from an unmerciful enemy, or put his faith in God even though the odds were so stacked that victory seemed impossible.

"I promise you," Kerry said, "that even now in this dark hour, God has not abandoned us. He will not leave us alone. That is a certainty."

Abe felt weak. He felt as if his mind were about to tear in two. "The enemy is so strong," he managed.

"Nothing is impossible with God. You must never forget that, Abe."

Panic boiled up inside him. He felt himself teetering on the proverbial ledge, about to topple into the dark waters of insanity.

"Look!" She grabbed him by the shoulders.

He stared into her dark eyes and felt himself fall into their depths.

She stared back intently. "You must decide to whom you will be loyal. If you choose the easy path and beg for mercy, your fate will be in their hands. I don't think you want that, do you?"

Abe shook his head.

"If you stay with us, you're staying by Jesus' side and even the gates of Hell will not be able to overcome us."

She let go of him and he staggered briefly. Her words left him dizzy.

Her piercing eyes left him speechless. Her words reverberated; he knew what she had said was true. He had to stay with the citizens of Geddon. There was no going back. He had already gone too far.

He stood tall and nodded to Kerry and Moses. Deep down, his fear still taunted him. He would need to fight that fear as best he could. He began to pray, hard. All the while, the hovercraft descended to Geddon. The engines hummed and kicked up the dust. The whirlwind was just beginning.

CHAPTER 80

Lucifer looked down on the town of Geddon. It was a far cry from the village that had once been too small for acknowledgment on maps and GPS. It had become very significant indeed. Its citizens filled the streets and outskirts, each and every one staring directly at him, each and every one armed for battle. That they were expecting him was no surprise. He had made no attempt to hide his coming.

He smiled. Although the town had grown into a metropolis, it was still the whole planet against this last bastion of the enemy. It wasn't even a question! He looked at his prophet and his smile broadened. Before the troops arrived, he wanted to entice any he could from the enemy's flock. If Bob's sugar didn't work, his army's vinegar would satisfy him almost as much.

He chuckled inwardly as he looked at his prophet. Good old Bob had been an asset. Too bad for him, this would be his last assignment. Once the town had been taken and the inhabitants had either joined them or been destroyed, there would be no more need for a prophet of the Ra—no more value to poor old Bob Gulam.

He probed Bob with his piercing stare. It would be a pleasure to possess this one, this last remaining believer in the great lie. He anticipated the moment when poor Bob finally saw the truth. By then, it would be too late. There would be no escaping his fate.

Lucifer turned his attention back to the window of the hovercraft and his prey. Out of the masses, he searched for one in particular. *Oh Kerry, you have eluded me for so long,* he thought. *But no more.*

Slowly the hovercraft descended to mere feet above the mass of Geddonites. He scanned the rabble with the eye of an eagle, looking for the one who had eluded him. He was so close to the Gatekeeper. He could *feel* it. He could almost taste her.

He continued, his hovercraft creeping along, scanning the inhabitants for that golden needle in the haystack. While he searched, he inhaled the intoxicants from the watchers below. He exhaled and his mood dimmed. It was good, but not great; less than he'd expected. Their terror-levels were a buzz-kill. He pacified himself, telling himself soon, *soon* they would fear him. Then he would feed upon them as he had never fed before.

There! He saw her standing with two others.

Elation reared in him, almost impossible to bear! He'd been searching for her so long, and now she stood right before him. She looked nothing as he remembered her from their last meeting. Then again, that was a very long time ago. She was no longer a child, but an elderly woman. Still, he could tell it was her. Her eyes gave her away—so dark, yet so full of light. He *hated* the light. He laughed out loud as he saw who stood beside her—Abe, would-be assassin turned double agent.

There was one other with her. He recognized this one by its odor. *Ah, the baby he was going to consume all of those years ago.* It looked as if he still had a chance to finish what he had started. *This day just keeps getting better,* he thought. *What a glorious day to end all days!*

The hovercraft roof retracted, leaving him in the open. He was not afraid of attack. His untethered powers rendered any attack harmless. He stood tall on the hovercraft that now served as a floating platform.

The old woman spoke into a microphone. Not only did it amplify through a loudspeaker, but it was apparently wired throughout the city so all the citizens could hear her, too. "Do not fear the one who comes. Stand firm to the end and you will be given a crown of life!"

He scoffed. So that was her game. Well, two could play. He used his untethered power. He touched his throat with the tips of his fingers, and tapped into the sound system. "Your leader is right. You have no need to fear me."

From the reaction of the masses, he knew they were hearing him. He continued. "I bring you opportunity for blessing. I am Lucifer, leader of the Ra. I come in peace."

The old woman glared at him with her deep eyes. She spoke into her microphone, not to the Geddonites, but to him. "You are the father of lies, Lucifer. You have no concern for men, but only for yourself. You are not the leader of the Ra. You are the leader of Hell." She almost growled the last word.

The hovercraft descended, lighting on the desert sands. He exited, Bob at his side. The crowd backed away, cowering before him. With a pained expression, he said. "What the old woman says is simply not true. I don't know if she is deliberately keeping you from my blessings, or if she is that ignorant. I know nothing of hell. In all the travels of the Ra, we have never encountered a heaven or a hell. Neither have we met demons or angels or gods. In truth, these entities and locations *do not exist.*"

"Do not listen to him!" The woman called to the Geddonites. "He is the Master of Lies!"

Lucifer held up his hands, palms out, a sign of peace. "We're getting nowhere," he said gently. "If you won't listen to me, listen to one of your own, who has been with me since the beginning and experienced first-hand the blessings I bestow on those who put their trust in the Ra." He indicated Bob. "Tell your story. Let them hear the truth from your own lips."

*

For years Bob had preached the truth, and yet he could not recall ever being so on edge as he was at that moment. Then again, he had never preached to such a tribe of stone-cold faces. Those faces reminded him of the stoic expressions that donned the giant faces of Easter Island.

Bob cleared his throat and realized he'd been given the same power as Lucifer. His voice carried through the enemy's sound system, through some Ra technology which never ceased to amaze him. He looked at them as his enemy. They had waited too long and deserved no mercy.

He glanced at Lucifer. The decision to show mercy was not his and his boss made no indication of changing plans. So, he would preach one last time to these stiff-necked people and hope none would come to their senses; then mercy would be a moot point.

"Look at me," he began knowing they already were looking. "I am over a century old. The Ra has given me immortality."

"Immortality is not a gift unless it is with God!" the old woman shouted. "You have sold your soul to Satan!"

Bob glanced at Lucifer who gestured to him to continue. Bob obeyed.

"Such gifts are bestowed upon those who put their faith in the Ra."

He paused and glared at the woman. She remained quiet, though her brown eyes shrieked at him with their intense stare. It was all he could do to remain focused on what needed to be said. "I know your lives have been burdened. I know you blame the Ra for your hardships, but deep down, you know your hardships were caused by your own stubbornness. If you would only acknowledge the Ra as the only entities akin to gods and goddesses, your lives would change for the better."

Bob grinned. A few in the crowd began to stir, the first signs their defenses were cracking. All he had to do was to push and pull until the cracks widened and the defenses fell.

In compromise to his benefactors, he would be okay with a few coming over—as long as it wasn't too many. He wanted plenty available for the final solution. What fun would it be if they all simply joined the ranks and received their marks? Regardless of his desires, he knew he must try to persuade the Geddonites. These were his orders, straight from Lucifer.

"There are two sides to every coin," he said. "Now is your last chance to be on the right side. An army is coming. It will be here soon, any minute. I have seen them and they are mighty. I have come ahead of them to warn you. This is your last chance. Come to us. Receive the mark of the Ra and live. Come before it is too late. If you don't, you will die."

His last words reverberated throughout the speaker system and disintegrated into a crackly silence. It was a silence so intense it could be felt, a wet wool blanket holding in a suffocating heat. He looked at his leader, hoping it was satisfactory to him. Then he looked out to the crowd of Geddon.

At first nothing happened. Then, one man struggled through the masses of the town. He fell before the hovercraft, trembling. A few more straggled forward. Maybe more would have come, but Bob felt certain the deep eyes of the old woman made many hesitate. She watched. She stared. Surprisingly, she remained silent.

He grinned wider. Their hesitation was fine by him. He was thankful they felt the need to stay with the brown-eyed one. He yearned for a bloodbath. He had waited a long time and could hardly believe the moment of sacrifice had finally arrived.

Lucifer took a further step from the hovercraft. Bob followed, though he disliked leaving the safety of the craft. He watched as his great leader embraced the few grovelers at his feet, as if they were prodigal children. As Lucifer directed his new charges, they stepped up onto the hovercraft and the roof closed over them. The craft took off, taking the newest members of the Ra away to receive their marks.

Lucifer and Bob now stood alone against those who opposed him. And yet they were not alone. In the distance, the sound of moving troops could be heard; it grew louder by the moment. Bob stood tall and proud. The time for mercy had passed. The moment of the final solution had dawned.

CHAPTER 81

Those in the hovercraft sat close together upon the floor, Vinnie among them. Vinnie had struggled a long time concerning the whole point of living in Geddon. Now he made his stand; there was no turning back. It was pointless to remain in Geddon. He took the only logical choice and boarded the last train leaving town.

He shook his head as he thought of the name of his new masters: the Ra. Kerry said they were not who they claimed to be. She believed the Ra were demons in disguise. Now, he knew he had been bamboozled, charmed by that old snake oil saleswoman. He would be scammed no longer!

He didn't know what to think of the Ra exactly. Maybe they were holding secrets, maybe they weren't. Honestly, he had quit caring. It didn't matter what they were. They were going to destroy Geddon. He was saving his own skin and anyone stupid enough to stay in that town was just plain bat-shit crazy.

He looked at the others with him. Fewer than ten had followed his lead. It stood as testimony to the general level of brainwashing the old woman had forced upon them. He understood how easy it was to buy into Kerry's ideology. He had done so himself. He felt fortunate his new masters had given this final opportunity. He was glad he'd taken it. The others with him didn't look as confident. They looked downright glum.

"Cheer up guys!" Vinnie tried for up-beat but was surprised to hear his own voice waiver with hesitation.

A few looked at him. The rest looked away. No one responded.

"Wow, tough crowd!" He tried to lighten the mood. "Why did the Geddonite cross the road?"

No one responded.

"To stay alive."

Silence.

"Oh come on guys, I just now came up with that one."

More silence.

"Geez, I'll be here all weekend. Don't forget to tip your waitress."

"Why don't you shut your cake-hole Vinnie."

Vinnie focused on the one who had spoken. "Glad to hear something from somebody. I thought I was on the wrong hovercraft for a second. This is the flight to better days right?"

"I said shut up. My wife stayed behind, for Pete's sake."

Vinnie shut up. He understood. He had no family, no ties to the place he'd just left. Now he realized that others may not have been so fortunate. He looked over the group. A few wiped tears from their cheeks. Others clenched their teeth together.

"Maybe we can convince the Ra to let our families live," a new voice chirped in. It was a young woman with fiery red hair.

Vinnie shared that sentiment, but he knew how things worked. "Look, I'm sorry. I really am, but they made their choices and we made ours. There's no point crying over spilled milk."

"Maybe we can ask the pilot to turn the craft around so we can convince them to come with us," Red said.

Vinnie shook his head. "I don't even know where the cockpit is on one of these things or who to ask. Plus, I have the feeling open enrollment to join this little club has closed permanently."

Red began to sob. "I left my boyfriend back there."

Vinnie wanted to console this woman, but could think of nothing to say. The hard truth was, if you weren't on this craft, you were as good as dead.

She sobbed. He put his arms around her. She pushed him away. "Oh, Steve." Steve was presumably her boyfriend's name. "Why didn't you come with me?"

Vinnie had always been a joker. Comedy was his wall behind which he hid in tense situations, but try as he might, he could find no humor here. That was probably a good thing. He certainly didn't need any help making himself more of an ass. There was no time to say more, anyway. The hovercraft landed with a gentle bump.

"Why did we land?" an older gentleman asked.

Red looked up from her hands. Her mascara had smeared. She looked like a raccoon. "We can't be far from Geddon," she mumbled. "We've only been traveling for a few minutes."

Vinnie assumed they were all going to Ra headquarters which he'd heard existed somewhere up in the Pacific Northwest. But, he realized, no one had actually told them they were headed there; it had just seemed logical. Everyone went there to get their marks of loyalty. Trying to keep positive, Vinnie spoke. "Probably engine trouble. Or maybe we're picking up more passengers."

Red's eyes brightened. "Maybe we've turned around. Maybe I can convince Steve?"

With a barely audible click, the roof retracted once again. The sun poured in through the opening. The former Geddonites stood up on the open platform. Vinnie looked. Vinnie gasped. He rubbed his eyes and looked again. This was no mirage.

"Oh my gosh," Red said in a whisper.

"I hope they're on our side," said another.

Vinnie stared at the army that was passing by them on all sides. The troops of the Ra stretched as far as could be seen. He was glad he had left when he did because now more than ever, Geddon didn't stand a chance.

"As long as we're here and not in Geddon, they won't harm us. They'll see we're on their craft. They'll know we're on their side." He needed to convince himself as much as the others.

"How do you know?" one of the group stuttered.

Before Vinnie could answer, the one who asked dropped to the floor, impaled through the skull. Vinnie gasped, unbelieving. A giant snake-like thing had shot out of the sky and skewered the man like a rabbit on a spit.

The others screamed as the impaled one's brains splatted upon them, but their voices cut off abruptly as the snakes shot through their skulls. A searing pain shot through Vinnie's head. As his world went dark, he saw the truth. He wished he had remained in Geddon. He wished with all of his might, but for him it was too late.

*

JoAnne's body rode her mount in regal fashion. It was easy, though she'd never before ridden such an animal. Her possessor, Splinter, had such expertise. She was but the puppet he controlled.

Her terror was exquisite and had been ever since she'd learned the truth. Now she knew, she wished she didn't. Life was so much better believing the demons were nothing more than the benevolent Ra. Over the time of her possession, Splinter had instructed her most thoroughly and cruelly about the Ra's demonic guise. Now, she saw a scene before her that intensified her terror further. A hovercraft had landed before them. The top had opened, exposing the passengers. Then they were no more.

She knew what had happened to them. Splinter kept nothing back. Indeed, he enjoyed telling her the truth at all times, now that escape was impossible. The beast had fed on them. And now, the beast was strong enough to completely cross the space between.

An end had come, but for JoAnne, this end would not provide her with relief, but only eternal pain and suffering. JoAnne began to cry.

CHAPTER 82

"And the sun should be turned into darkness, and the moon into blood." – Acts 2:20

*

Kerry stood before the Devil. Her heart broke. She had witnessed the hovercraft's exodus. Only a handful chose to leave. Still, for her, even one was too many. She watched them get into the hovercraft; watched them depart knowing she would never see them again. She didn't want them to leave. They'd already suffered so much and now they weren't to finish the race? Very sad. She knew she couldn't make decisions for them. No one stayed in Geddon a captive. Everyone had free will.

She stared at the ridge that the lost had disappeared over and forced her lamentations away. There was no time to lament. Not many had chosen to leave. Most remained. This was her flock, the 144,000 of Geddon, give or take a few. It was them against the world.

She looked from the ridge to the king of this world, Lucifer—the Devil. She stared him in the eyes, refusing to let fear be her master. She was prepared to stare down evil indefinitely, but she suddenly felt dizzy. She stumbled back into the arms of Abe and Moses. "Do you hear that?" She asked.

Abe and Moses nodded.

"What is it?" she asked. She saw nothing, but felt a sickening bombardment of blasphemies hit her like a full-throttled freight train.

"I don't know," Abe said. His voice sounded strangely distant.

"I know." Moses' voice came to her through the blasphemous tidal wave. "It's the beast! It's coming!"

Moses' words triggered her memories of the creature from her nightmare. She remembered the beast murdering the people of Outer Earth. She shuddered.

Above the din of the blasphemies, she heard the Devil's laugh echo through the speaker system of Geddon and into her ears like a spreading cancer. As if the beast and the Devil were not enough, flashes of lighting split the clear-blue sky. Instinctively she shielded her eyes, watching it. What she saw released her fears into the wild of her mind. She recognized those flailing appendages. The beast was breaking through the Space

Between—and not just its serpent-like heads. No, it was pushing all the way through.

Despite her promises to herself, Kerry screamed. It was beyond her control, the terror overwhelming. The light of day dimmed as the sky ripped and the beast emerged, bursting out into her world in grotesque birth.

The day grew dim, dim enough for the moon to show itself, blood-red in the twilight-sky. Kerry fought for steadiness. Between the blasphemies of the beast, the cackles of the Devil, and the changing of the sky; she teetered on the edge of sanity. She cried out to her God to save her. She begged. She pleaded. Lucifer laughed. The sun grew dark. The beast had arrived!

CHAPTER 83

The Geddonites watched as the beast made its dramatic entry. Lucifer used the distraction to focus on Bob Gulam. The time of truth had arrived. He drew the one who had served him so well; very near. "Well, Bob," he said, with a broad smile. "It looks like your job is no longer needed."

Bob backed away. Fear glimmered in his eyes; the color vanished from his skin.

Lucifer inhaled. The terror rolling off Bob was intoxicating, a thousand sticks of incense burning on a heathen altar. He stuck out his tongue as if trying to catch a snowflake. He caught more than snowflakes, so much more. He savored the terror in the air. He would enjoy possessing Bob.

The First Seeker stumbled backwards, barely staying on his feet, his eyes locked on Lucifer. "Have I not served the Ra well?"

Lucifer nodded. "You have."

"Have I not brought the masses to you?" Bob stammered.

Lucifer nodded again. "You have done your job well, my good and faithful servant."

"Why are you displeased, then, Lord Lucifer? I've given my all to you."

Lucifer grinned. He appreciated Bob's efforts at self-preservation. "No. You have not given me your all. Not yet."

"Please tell me, what I have done to displease you?"

Lucifer answered with a chuckle. "You have not displeased me in the least. It is simply your time to know the truth about what you have put your faith in." Lucifer seized him. In an instant they were one flesh. Lucifer enjoyed this part the most. He felt Bob squirm and twist, trying to escape.

"No! It can't be!" Bob shrieked.

"Oh, it is." Lucifer held Bob firmly, enjoying his writhing. "You see who the Ra is and always have been and always will be. You've chosen poorly who to give your loyalties to, my dear friend."

"No," Bob said again, but this time with less defiance.

Bob swung at Lucifer. Lucifer released his prisoner, not so he could get away, but for the fun of watching him try. Bob retreated into the farthest reaches of himself, but Lucifer was there waiting.

"You can't get away," he hissed, "not with the choices you've made. You are mine, forever."

Bob let out a shriek. It made Lucifer giddy with elation.

The demon king laughed. "Take pride, dear Bob, I saved you for last."

CHAPTER 84

"And behold a great red dragon, having seven heads and ten horns, and seven crowns upon its heads. And his tail drew the third part of the stars of heaven, and did cast them to the earth." – Revelation 12:4.

*

The beast emerged completely into view. And what a view it was.

In the dim light a few stars still shone—not brightly, but they were visible. Perhaps two-thirds couldn't be seen. Either the massive beast blocked the rest from view, or they lacked the energy to shine.

The hole through which the beast had come remained open, revealing a desolate place of ruins and death

With the appearance of this newcomer, Abe forgot to keep his eyes on Lucifer. Now he searched him out and realized he was nowhere to be found. Panic set in. As a defector to Geddon, he must always be on guard against his old master. Yet he'd so quickly forgotten.

Shame dwelt within Abe. With the last offer to board the hovercraft, he'd almost caved. He knew the power of this enemy. He'd witnessed the killings in the room with the drain. He'd resisted the temptation to board the hovercraft, but only barely. He credited his standing firm on Kerry's acts.

Kerry had shown him the light. He knew what the Ra were. That knowledge had kept him from groveling at the enemy's feet. Going back was not an option. He felt Kerry grab his hand. He looked at her and knew this was where he belonged. No matter what happened, he was a Geddonite.

Lucifer was absent, but his little stooge was there. Abe scoffed at this one—the Ra's prophet, the one who, under orders from Lucifer had abused him in the room with the drain. But this one looked different somehow. He exhibited an air of authority as if he no longer took orders, but gave them. He approached the beast with confidence, and raised his hands. The beast approached him with equal confidence.

The blasphemous bombardment from the creature intensified as the two drew together. Lucifer's prophet stood before the beast. Then he was no more. With one great movement, the beast threw the prophet into the gaping hole in its front. It was a ragged hole; a wound, however, that didn't seem to affect the creature.

It tossed the prophet into itself and immediately, its appearance changed. It glowed red, as red as the blood moon that hovered behind it. The ragged wound healed and disappeared.

That can't be good, Abe thought.

With its feast, the monster seemed stronger. It seemed wiser.

Again, Abe felt the urge to leave Geddon, to beg for mercy from the beast, but his feet would not move. Doubt urged him forward, but terror held him back. Terror proved the stronger, but not by much. It was more than the terror of what the beast would do to him if he stayed in Geddon. It was the terror of what the beast might do to him if he ran to it.

It was too late to ask for forgiveness from this enemy. He didn't want to. The fear was immense within him, but so was his new-found faith. He was a new creation and couldn't go back to what he had been. Fear and faith waged a bitter war in him. He wrestled with himself. To go or not to go—it was tearing him apart.

*

Moses trembled. He had a theory, but it didn't seem to hold now. His father had OCD and that debilitation turned out to be a great asset on the opposite side of the Space Between. He'd inherited the OCD. But here, on this side of the Space Between, he had wondered if his strength would be magnified. He'd wondered if he was called to be Geddon's champion.

Now, as he stared up at the beast towering over him, glowing like the blood moon that hovered above it, he questioned his theory. The beast was so big, so powerful. Blasphemies boomed from it, making it hard to concentrate; to keep his theory intact.

He stepped forward one step. It was a hard step, almost impossible, but he did it. Then he took a second. The second was easier than the first. Then another. Then another. Then another. He was running now. The distance between the beast and himself closed. *One, two, three. One, two, three. One two, three.* He hoped his theory was sound.

He counted. He ran. He didn't know if his speed was increasing to super-human levels. He shoved fear away, preparing himself for battle.

*

The Devil shrieked with excitement as he entered the beast. Bob shrieked in horror. Lucifer loved being inside the beast. It had become a dragon, now he was one with it. He stared out at the slime of Geddon through the dragon's eyes. How he would love destroying this last vestige of the enemy!

"Ha!" He laughed through the dragon's great and terrible vocal chords. Then he saw one coming at him—the son of the one he had fought previously. This time the victor would be him. His power was untethered. This human was no match.

The man raced fast, his legs nearly flying. Lucifer drew back his great dragon head, hissing, and reared to meet him. The great last battle was about to begin!

CHAPTER 85

JoAnne jostled about on the mount she and her possessor rode. It was a crowded ride, two souls and one body. The dust that hung in the air, stirred up by the thousands marching and riding, the sulfuric stench rolling off her mount, the sway of her steed, and the suffocating stuffiness inside her own self made her want to vomit. Her sense of hopelessness didn't help.

Bile burned her throat like a hot branding iron. She swallowed it back. She would not disgrace the uniform she wore. Her face still throbbed from the last time she had defiled it. She learned, that day, that Splinter didn't take well to such things. He had used her own battle-helmet as a bludgeoning weapon. Her own arm had dealt the blows. She had lost teeth. She had lost blood. She had lost her last ounce of will.

*

Strangely, though, as she fell to the floor that horrible day, taking her punishment, she had seen a vision. She saw the reflection of a man, staring at her from a dirty mirror. She was the man, seeing the reflection through his eyes. Blood covered his face and trickled from his mouth.

Through his eyes, she looked down. Crimson droplets of blood speckled the public restroom floor on which the man stood. Bits of white and red were scattered about the floor. She looked back up into the mirror. The man's open mouth showed missing teeth. Something swayed in her peripheral vision. She saw. The man held a blood-stained motorcycle helmet.

The vision faded. Now, she was just JoAnne, still being beaten. She begged him to stop, but her words were indecipherable, her lips swollen, her front teeth gone, her nose broken. The pain was intense.

He bashed her two more times. "What fun," she heard her possessor hiss within her soul. "I haven't had that much fun since the possession of Levi Burke." As she blacked out, she heard Splinter's last words. "Thanks for the memories, baby."

*

The memories of that beating stuck with her. It had only been a few days, but she would have remembered it if it had been a thousand lifetimes ago. She felt Splinter jostling within her, a life-sucking leach. She could hear him laughing and knew his jostling was intentional. She couldn't escape his taunts. Still, she forced the vomit back. The nightmare of that beating was not something she wanted repeated, at any cost.

She wished for death. Except, wasn't she already living a death every moment she existed with this demon. How could she die when already dead? She shuddered.

Together, they crested a ridge and the sight she saw brought her out of her delirium. She beheld the legendary city of Geddon. It was bigger than she had imagined. Still, it was nothing compared to the forces converging on it. The Geddonites were outnumbered thousands to one. A great dragon towered above them. She could sense Lucifer within the dragon, along with Bob. Splinter allowed that much knowledge.

She squinted, straining to see. The unnatural dimness of the day made it difficult. But it seemed one of the Geddonites was challenging Lucifer, the great dragon. He ran full-speed. She pitied him. He still had hope. She despised knowing she would soon see that hope crushed.

The man shouted a war-cry and at the same moment, the dragon's great foot went up into the air. No, it wasn't a war-cry. He was counting.

The dragon's foot came down. The counting man was silenced.

CHAPTER 86

Abe stared at the abomination before them, causing devastation. It seemed unreal. None of it was happening, he argued with himself. It couldn't be. But he knew it was. He'd heard stories of the strength of Moses' father. He'd hoped to see God work through this warrior. That hope died as the dragon's massive foot descended. A plume of desert sand erupted as it crashed to the arid land. The dust settled. The dragon remained. Moses was gone.

The blasphemies multiplied ten-fold. Abe tried to block them out, but they screamed to him not only from the outside, but from within him as well. The dragon spoke directly to him, telling him how foolish he'd been to defect, telling him what his future held—terror, pain. Abe shook his head, denying. But out there on the battlefield, the David of Geddon had been slain. The giant remained.

Beyond the giant, in the strange twilight dimness of mid-day, he saw movement. At first, it seemed as if the desert itself had come to life, rippling everywhere as far as the eye could see and drawing nearer with every second.

Abe squinted into the sands, and suddenly the truth revealed itself. Countless troops approached, each one wearing supernatural armor, each one riding supernatural mounts. Lucifer's voice echoed, but he couldn't tell if it was in his own mind, or if everyone heard. *We are the Ra? No, the old woman was right. We are demons. She told you the truth.*

Abe staggered and trembled.

What the old woman didn't tell you is this: you have no chance of survival unless you bow to me. Bow to me and I may yet show mercy.

Abe howled and clawed at his face. He wished he had not come to Geddon. He wished he had died back in the room with the drain.

Come to me! Bow to me!

But a smaller voice spoke to him as well. It came from within himself, murmuring to stay put, stay with the Geddonites, with God's people. It sounded so far away, barely audible beside the booming shrieks.

Come back to me! Lucifer shouted. *Come back to me!*

Lucifer's booming words overpowered the small voice. Abe trembled. He shook. He sobbed, but he made no move one way or the other.

The dragon lifted its foot. Stuck to the underside, was Moses—or what was left of him.

Abe sobbed harder.

*

Kerry watched the battle from beginning to abrupt finish. She felt the shock wave as the dragon's clawed foot landed. She witnessed the murder of Moses. *At least it was quick and painless,* she thought as tears welled in her brown eyes. She didn't know how God was going to rescue them now. She had thought it would come through Moses as it had previously come through his father. That hope was dashed.

The blasphemous words shouted by the great dragon grew deafening. Covering her ears did nothing to stop it, as it seemed to come from within herself, reminding her of her sinfulness.

"Sinful or not, I am redeemed by the blood of the lamb!" she shouted with all the resolve she could muster.

The blasphemies stopped. In its place, Lucifer called from the mouth of the great red dragon. "Stupid woman!" The voice came low and croaking through the dragon's crimson lips. "You say you are redeemed. Where *is* your redeemer? Who will save you from my coming wrath?"

Kerry remained silent. She knew the answer—but suddenly she couldn't form the words, couldn't pull her thoughts together.

The dragon smiled. "Listen to me, Geddonites, I know who among you believes they have been redeemed. I know who doesn't."

"Don't listen," Kerry shouted over the PA system. But her voice sounded small, weak, unsure compared to Satan's.

"Ah," the dragon chuckled. "Here is a true believer, but her belief is based on fairy tales. She'll never believe the truth. She'll never accept that she's been buying into fables all her life."

"We will not be swayed by *you,* Satan!" she retorted.

The dragon inhaled. The dragon blew a white fire.

Kerry burned, and Geddon burned with her.

CHAPTER 87

"One shall be taken and the other left." – Matthew 24:40

*

Abe fell face down as dragon-fire engulfed Geddon. The heat was excruciating. He yearned for God to save him, but the words of the dragon rang in his ears. *I know who truly believes that they have been redeemed. I also know who of you does not.* Abe's doubt in his own redemption raged. He screamed for mercy. He begged. He was heard not by the lamb, but by the dragon. Mercifully, the heat diminished.

He cried. He wailed. He kept his face buried in the desert sand.

"Get up," he heard the dragon say.

He obeyed.

He got up. He looked about. The devastation was complete.

Geddon was no more. The buildings were nothing but piles of rubble. Much of the desert sand had been transformed into glass. Most of the inhabitants of the city had been vaporized. Strangely though, not all of them had perished. A few had survived, seemingly unscathed. Kerry was gone. Not a bone fragment or charred fleck of dust remained of her.

"I wanted to do away with you all!" the dragon's voice overwhelmed Abe. "But I relented and spared a few. Do you know why?"

Abe didn't answer. Neither did any of the others with him.

"I know your thoughts. I know you doubted the lies of the old woman. There is no redeemer. There is no savior; no lamb who was slain. There is only me!"

A few people whimpered. Others wept openly.

The dragon roared, shaking its head; the mighty sound silenced all.

"I spared you," the dragon shouted, "because I am merciful. You who doubted the saving grace of your messiah must now choose. Choose me and you will live. Choose the way of the other Geddonites and you will share in their destruction."

Abe struggled. Yes, the Ra were demons. But where was the champion, Jesus, who was promised to come and save them? Kerry had put her faith in Him, and her end had been complete and final.

"All who wish to live, come to me!" The dragon's voice echoed in Abe's ears and heart.

Some staggered through the ash and blackened bones toward the demonic forces. Others, though, held their ground. Conflict raged in Abe. He had already joined the demons once on the promise of a better life. Instead, he had witnessed brutal death and been driven into the desert to commit murder.

The Geddonites, by contrast, had rescued him, nursed him back to health. They had shown him mercy. They had *been* Christ's hands and feet of whom they spoke.

And then there was his vision. It was only days ago he had felt so drawn into being baptized into the name of the lamb, to be protected from the beast. He looked up at the terrorizing abomination before him. There was no shame, he thought, in fearing one that wielded such power.

Abruptly, a verse popped into his head, from the Bible he'd been studying. *Do not be afraid of those who kill the body, but cannot kill the soul. Rather, be afraid of the one who can destroy both body and soul in hell.*

He said this more to himself than to those around him. The dragon was the one referred to in that scripture, the one who could destroy both body and soul. As he stood frozen, moving neither toward nor away from the dragon, more scripture popped into his thoughts. His legs wanted to run to the one he feared, but the verses held him still.

For God so loved the world that he gave his only Son, that whoever believes in him, should not perish, but have eternal life. This Son was the lamb who had been slain. He believed. He just couldn't understand why the lamb wasn't helping him now.

Whoever believes is not condemned, but whoever does not believe stands condemned already. The voice grew stronger. He couldn't tell if it was his own thoughts, or something more. Either way, the path was becoming clear.

He looked about. Some were standing their ground. Others were going to the enemy. "Stop!" He yelled, barely realizing his outburst. "Stay in Geddon! Trust in the God who saves!"

A few stopped. One looked at him. Another shook his head and kept walking. The first who had looked turned back and stood by Abe. She trembled, but she stopped. The other fled into the ranks of the enemy. Some followed him, while others rallied around Abe. The sides had been chosen. The choices became final. Abe stood his ground with the remnant. He felt overwhelming calmness. He had sealed his fate. Time would show what that fate was.

With a low growl, the dragon spoke to his demonic forces. "Destroy the filthy remnant of Geddon."

*

Lucifer felt ready to burst with ecstasy as he watched his army advance. He lifted his dragon head to the bloody moon and laughed.

His pleasure was overwhelming. His senses were peeked, tingling with stimulation. The high was exquisite. His troops were wonderful, each mortal giving off a powerful scent of terror, each possessed by at least one demon. He soaked in the cries of the possessed, their souls begging for mercy, and laughed, drinking in the glorious cocktail of gratification.

Yet, there was a taste of bitters in the cocktail. It was smothering his buzz. He searched for the source of this bitterness. It took only a moment to zero in on it. He flickered out his forked tongue, tasting the air.

Yes—the bitterness emanated from the remnant of Geddon. He glared at them, enraged that they defiled his moment of victory. They were few indeed, standing there in a huddle, praying. *Damn them! They were praying!*

Typical, he thought. He hated this last speck of believers. He hated them with a fury, a passion! But he forced a grin. They would be gone from his presence soon enough. Even now, his forces were entering the ruins as the remnant inched further into the center of the former metropolis.

A particularly strong gust of their vile prayers hit him. It was repulsive, like vomit hitting his face. They crowded into the center of the ruins. His forces converged from all sides. Lucifer's smile grew. Soon those vile prayers would be silenced. *Patience Lucifer,* he chastised himself. But it was so hard. Those prayers were awful. He could feel those pleas sticking to him like blood-sucking leaches. The bitterness would end, any moment now. Still, their words of prayer were torturous.

In his rage, he bombarded the prayerful with the full wrath of his blasphemies, his explosive expletives. Despite all his efforts, their prayers continued. *Damn them!* he raged. *Damn them!*

*

Abe had gathered the few who remained, to pray. It was all they could do. The dragon's blasphemies snaked into his ears. *Focus,* he ordered himself, as he continued leading the group in prayer. *Focus.* But Satan's expletives wriggled past his defenses, bitter as wormwood.

He took consolation with the growing awareness that the demons seemed to hate the prayers. Lucifer's blasphemies gave evidence of this. If the demons hated it, he must ensure the prayers didn't stop. He joined hands with the last few, praying harder, praying louder. The blasphemies died down as he focused in on the one to whom he prayed, the lamb who had been slain.

For a second, the blasphemies disappeared. Then, they rebounded, hitting him with unbearable force, a great scream of perversion. He took the brunt of it, staggering back, but shouting out his prayers even louder. Those with him did the same.

They prayed as they retreated deeper into the ruins. The once magnificent buildings of Geddon were reduced to smoldering ash. Not one stone stood upon another. The enemy closed in on them from every direction, their circle of safety shrinking steadily. He prayed with all his heart.

Lucifer continued to chip away. Abe could feel it. He vowed to remain unbroken, pushing back the bitterness of the Devil's schemes. The vow felt hollow. Still, he refused to backtrack. He would not doubt his belief. His faith would not waiver again. With a flash, he recalled Peter's words, when he was given the option to leave his savior. *Lord, to whom shall we go? You have the words of eternal life.*

He looked around. No savior could be seen, but where else would they go? They continued to pray. They prayed. They prayed. *They prayed!*

The enemy tightened the circle around them, like a vice of hardened steel, cranked notch by notch, tighter and tighter, squeezing those within its trap. Abe prayed so hard the sweat on his brow felt thick as blood as it slid down his face.

*

JoAnne and Splinter rode in on the first wave. Black ash and charred ruins was all that remained of the once grand town.

The advancing troops were no longer shiny in their armor, but coated with the ash that had been kicked up in clouds by the movement of the troops. Splinter loved this land where darkness had fallen. It was glorious—and most detrimental to poor JoAnne. She coughed and sputtered as she breathed in the haze. He loved her pain. Every bit she endured, he enjoyed.

Ahead, Splinter could see the scurrying of those about to be annihilated. He spurred JoAnne's heart to race as his excitement grew. He relished the coming final victory over the enemy. He felt JoAnne squirm within and among him. "What's the matter, little imp?"

She didn't respond, but he knew. He felt her revulsion. He sensed her disdain. He tasted her depression, her hopelessness. It was most savory upon his pallet. He guided their mount ever closer to the enemy. He could see them now through the dust. They were in full retreat. He smiled with malice. Their escape route was being cut off. They were surrounded and the circle was tightening around them like a noose upon the convicted.

JoAnne was trying not to look. He forced her to watch. "What's the matter, JoAnne? After all the time you've spent with me, you've lost your taste for blood? Is that it?"

Still no answer. She tried harder to turn away; he overrode her attempt. "You'll see far more disturbing things than this, my little imp. You'll see things beyond your ability to imagine."

"No. Please," she begged.

"What did you expect? You sided with Satan. You sold your soul."

She whimpered.

Splinter laughed, giddy with delight. Only one thing soured his mood. *They were praying. Those damned Geddonites were praying!* He hated that.

Onward and forward. He pushed his mount towards them. Despite the bitter air that wafted to him from the prayerful, he forced himself forward. He had orders, and orders from Lucifer were to be obeyed, no excuses.

Onward. The massacre must commence. Onward.

*

Without Kerry and Moses, it seemed Abe had become the leader by default. He wasn't sure how or why—he was the newest to Geddon after all, a mere infant in his faith. On the heels of this thought came a verse. *The first will be last and the last will be first.* And, *anyone who does not receive the kingdom of God like a little child, will never enter it.*

Now, as the forces of darkness encroached, he led the few survivors in prayer. He looked over the small group as they bowed their heads in obedience to a savior who had promised to be with them to the very end of the age. There were men. There were children. There were women. People of every race were represented. Even a few of the tall pale people were there, refugees from a now-barren world.

It was quite odd to see. The remnant was armed. They had prepared for this battle. Yet now as the apocalypse drew close, they simply prayed.

Voices came to him as he prayed, conflicting voices, tugging at him for loyalty. The inner voice whispered, *I am with you always to the very end of the age.* "Ha!" countered the voice of the great dragon. "He says he'll be with you to the end of the age? Where is this great savior of yours, then? He must be around here somewhere. Maybe he's sleeping. Pray harder. Pray louder. Maybe he'll wake up and save you!"

It disturbed Abe to feel the dragon could hear the voice within him.

I am with you always. Even at the very end of the age.

"Come to us you worthless creatures. You can be our slaves since your messiah seems to have abandoned you."

I am with you always. Even at the very end of the age. With great difficulty, Abe shunned the dragon's taunts and focused on the voice within. It was so difficult. The enemy was loud. The enemy was bold. The enemy was relentless.

Yet, that inner voice persisted. *I am with you always. Even to the very end of the age.*

Abe continued to lead the prayer, the Geddonites joining in as the Dragon roared and Hell's army drew nearer. He raised his head, seeing the abomination coming for them! "Jesus!" He screamed against the torrent. "Save us!"

Hell's army was now so close he could feel the heat of their damned bodies as their millions pressed in. Their mounted troops terrified him. "Jesus! Save us! Please!" The remnant of Geddon huddled amidst the hoards of Hell, circling about them in a vortex of evil.

The dragon leapt high into the air, then soared down on the Geddonites. Abe looked up at its terrible wings, spread to blot out even the dim sun. Everything slowed. The end was near! The dragon came. "Jesus, save us," he shouted one last time.

Time expired. It was finished.

Lord to whom shall we go, you have the words of eternal life. Those words froze within his mind as Abe waited with head bowed and eyes shut.

CHAPTER 88

"And I saw heaven opened, and behold a white horse; and he that sat upon him was called Faithful and True, and in righteousness he doth judge and make war." – Revelation 19:11

*

A great thunder ripped suddenly through the sky, stopping Lucifer, frozen, only inches from destroying the last remnant of Geddon. For a moment, he hung in the air, just out of feasting range. His forked tongue caressed the hair on Abe's head. He salivated, straining for his victim. Then he was being pulled back, dragged away from them.

At first, Lucifer was confused. Then he saw. His confusion evaporated. Rage filled the void, a white-hot rage.

*

"His eyes were as a flame of fire, and on his head were many crowns." – Revelation 19:12

*

Abe felt different. Something had rustled his hair, just for a moment, leaving him cold as death. It only lasted a moment though. As he prayed, the chill dissipated, leaving in its place a warmth which he felt from the top of his head to the depth of his very soul. He looked up, expecting to see the gaping jaws of the dragon. What he actually saw was quite unexpected.

The dragon hovered high in the sky. Abe stared in disbelief. The dragon was not alone. There was another—a great man riding a great white horse hovered there with him in the sky, fitted for battle. The rider wore many crowns, a true King of Kings and Lord of Lords.

The dragon thrust its chest out, shouting at the rider, but either nothing came from its terrible lips, or his words couldn't be heard over the great thunder of the Lord.

Abe fell to his knees, with all the rest—and not just the survivors of Geddon, but the entire army of Hell. Abe remembered another of his newly-learned scriptures. *Every knee shall bow.*

*

"And I saw the beast, and the kings of the earth, and their armies, gathered together to make war against him that sat on the horse." – Revelation 19:19.

*

Lucifer raged. He would not be defeated again! He mustered his courage and reared, large and powerful. He shook the desert with a roar from the dragon's throat. "My powers have been untethered," he shouted at the rider. "Fight and die!"

What angered Lucifer the most was the fear he felt. Even with all the untethered powers of Hell mustered within him, he felt fear. He fought the urge to go to his knees as all the rest had. He would not do it! He pushed his fears away, and roared. "I said fight or die!!"

The one on the horse said nothing.

"Will you not accept my challenge?" The other's silence was infuriating.

The rider stared silently at the dragon.

"You haven't changed a bit have you?" Lucifer taunted. He circled the horseman. "I recall another time, not so long ago, when you were being taunted by your own high priests. I seem to remember you remaining silent then as well."

The horseman remained still as stone. His horse, however, twitched its ivory body as if it could wait no longer to charge. Horse and rider alike stared down the dragon with piercing eyes.

The anger grew in Lucifer. He forced back a stare of his own, the unholy trinity of Lucifer, the dragon and the prophet. "My powers are untethered," he said. "Don't you realize I can destroy this remnant of Geddon with a mere thought? I can destroy even you if I so wish?"

The horseman spoke. "You are right, Lucifer."

Lucifer stood even taller in his dragon-body. He knew he was right, but it felt good to hear it from God's own son.

The horseman added, "You are right in saying I haven't changed."

The dragon continued to circle around the rider, searching for any trickery.

"I remember I remained silent in the faces of the high priests, but do you remember what I said to Pilate?"

"I don't *care*," Lucifer spat.

"Pilate was much like you are now. He felt his power over me. Do you remember that day? He was drunk with the delusion of his own power. He said, as you say now, that he had the authority to have me killed."

Lucifer did not like where this was going. He snarled, but said nothing.

"I know you remember my response that day. It was an important day—the day I was sentenced to be crucified."

Lucifer let out a war-cry. The cry angered him. In his own ears it sounded more like a child's tantrum. He trembled with rage.

"I told Pilate he would have no power over me had it not been given to him from above."

Lucifer's eyes blazed. "My power is untethered! You cannot change that. These are the words written in the prophecies!"

"I am the word! The living word! The word made flesh!"

The voice hit Lucifer like the pressure wave from a bomb's detonation.

"You are darkness," the horseman said, "as I am light! As darkness, you cannot understand me any more than you can understand the ancient scriptures!"

Lucifer glanced back at his forces. They waited, still in formation, although their knees were bowed. He wondered if they would obey him if he ordered them to rise and charge.

The horseman turned and looked at the Geddonites, on their knees as well. "And I quote from the holy scriptures 'to those who believe in me, I give the right to become children of God.' And 'those who are faithful unto death, I will give the crown of life.'"

Lucifer saw his advantage. While the horseman's back was turned, he struck. He moved in, silent as the night and quick as a serpent.

CHAPTER 89

JoAnne saw the dragon advance and knew the horseman was oblivious to the danger. Despite the sacrilege, she thought it was a cowardly move.

The instant the thought escaped, she wished it hadn't. Splinter dealt out a punishment that left her dizzy with pain. "How dare you insult Lord Lucifer!" he shrieked within her possessed body.

She gritted her teeth together, but not before inadvertently capturing the tip of her tongue. Her teeth came together hard. Her tongue escaped her body in a torrent of crimson.

Jealousy surged through her as that tip fell away, the only part of her that was not under this yoke of slavery. With blood flowing down her chin, she begged Splinter to stop his punishment, the beating, the stings of unseen lashes. She felt faint and wished for the release of unconsciousness. As the world began to go dark, Splinter yanked her back.

"No you don't!" His voice echoed as if through a dark tunnel. "You are mine. You want the pain to stop?"

"Yes!" she shrieked with what tongue remained.

"Are you sure?"

"Yes! Yes, please!"

Splinter began to laugh. "I won't stop it. You can't stop it. Your eternal punishment will now begin in earnest." Splinter laughed harder. JoAnne gnashed her teeth in agony.

*

Abe watched the treachery unfold. His redeemer had turned his back on Satan! How could the Son of God make such a mistake? He wanted to look away. He couldn't stand to see his last strand of hope severed by the dragon. He tried to look away, but couldn't.

He watched in terror, wishing to warn his messiah, but it was happening too fast.

*

How had it happened that Bob Gulam had risen to such heights only to find himself plummeting into the depths? All this time he'd thought he was helping a higher power dispense grace, when in actuality, he'd been nothing but Satan's tool.

He felt stupid, now he knew the truth, and stupider still to learn he was the last to see it. Worse still, there could be no hope for his redemption. He had chosen his loyalties and he had chosen poorly. There was no way to turn back.

He wanted to hide from his possessor, but things were too cozy, the two of them in the dragon's body, to accomplish this. He suspected even if the land around him was wide and open, it wouldn't be enough. Satan would still have him, would still possess him, and now, he was an unwilling participant in a battle between this mysterious horseman with many crowns and his eternal master, Lucifer. It was a battle he didn't wish to be involved in, but his wishes were no longer his.

The horseman had turned his back, a critical mistake—whether of overconfidence, or stupidity, Bob didn't know.

The dragon struck with the speed of a viper and the silence of dead air. Bob tried to look away, but Lucifer disallowed it.

CHAPTER 90

Abe's mouth gaped, trying to warn the horseman. It was too late. In one gulp, the dragon consumed both horse and rider. He threw his head back, laughing. Abe's heart sank.

The dragon swung its head towards the huddling remnant. "Pledge your allegiance to me, or your suffering will be exquisite."

Abe was tempted. They were defeated. He didn't want to suffer. Still his knowledge of the enemy persisted. Demons were liars. He guessed they would inflict suffering regardless of his allegiance. Again, Peter's words came to mind. *Lord to whom shall we go? You have the words of eternal life.*

He wanted to surrender, be done. The words of the horseman echoed in his mind. *To those who are faithful unto death, I will give the crown of life.*

But who was left to be faithful to? he wondered. He took a tentative step toward the dragon. *The one who could give such a crown had been consumed by the dragon.*

"Yes." The dragon arched its head forward, salivating. "Come to me. Bow at my feet." He leered as Abe drew closer.

The dragon had consumed his only hope; still Abe struggled. Even though Jesus had been defeated, would it do him any more harm to remain loyal even unto death? He struggled with the choice before him.

"Come!" the dragon hissed. "Bow. *Beg for mercy.*"

Abe took another step forward. Around him, he saw the Devil's army rise from where they had knelt. The dragon's grin widened.

*

Splinter poked JoAnne, thrilled to see the final resistance unfold. JoAnne squealed as he poked harder. He relished her agony like a fine wine. He relished seeing Abe take another step. It was wonderful to see this one, especially, grovel. He let out a whoop and a holler through JoAnne's mouth. Whoops of elation spread to others of the possessed. Lucifer's army was ready to celebrate. He grabbed JoAnne by her soul and gave a celebratory twist. It was so much fun. It was wonderful.

*

Lucifer watched in glee. This stupid one was caving. Of course he had no intention of rewarding this idiot for his surrender. He would damn him to Hell just like all the rest who had abandoned Jesus.

He tormented Bob, squeezing his arms, his legs, his chest. Bob wailed as Lucifer crushed him. Lucifer delighted in Bob's pain. It was wonderful!

He looked at stupid little Abe taking yet another step toward him. "Bow before me, Human!" he shouted. "Perhaps I will forgive."

Abe bowed. The dragon grinned.

"Now pledge your allegiance and I will consider your offering."

Abe lifted his head. His words shook, as he said, "I pledge my allegiance to the only one who can save me now." Then he shouted, as loud as he could, "I pledge my allegiance to Jesus Christ!"

The dragon's grin disappeared. Flames blazed from Lucifer's eyes.

CHAPTER 91

JoAnne couldn't believe it. Even now, after the dragon had consumed the horseman, this Geddonite remained loyal to his messiah? *Inconceivable.* She looked over the remnant of the once great city. They all bowed, but not to Lucifer. They all pledged allegiance to Jesus Christ! *Absolutely inconceivable.*

The dragon's tail lashed, enraged by this final act of defiance. He rose and shrieked a command, his voice hoarse with anger. "Show no mercy to this scourge of my kingdom. Destroy them! Feast on their souls!"

In one mighty roar, the demonic army answered. "Yes, Lord Lucifer!"

They advanced as one, converging towards the praying remnant. Lucifer stood before them, the proud and mighty dragon; his crimson hide glistening in the dimmed light of a newly-dawning world, a true victor.

Although JoAnne thought the Geddonites were fools to resist, she sympathized. She tried to turn away from what she was about to witness, but Splinter cruelly yanked her back into line. "You will watch the slaughter," he shrieked within her.

"Please don't make me," she begged.

"You'll see far worse in the coming ages," he spat at her from within herself.

She struggled to push away her captor, but Splinter's grip was solid. "You are mine to torment! You're mine for eternity!"

She stopped resisting. There was no point. There was no hope, none at all.

*

Abe stood his ground as did the others. The dragon approached with his unholy army close on its heels. It rose up, let out a great roar, and readied itself to strike the final blow. Abe could do nothing but wait to witness his own demise.

*

Something was happening that didn't make sense. Lucifer felt a twinge of fear inside himself, small and insignificant, but growing by the second, a cancer. He was ready to strike the remnant. He should have no fear, yet fear stalled him. He hesitated.

Something was amiss. *What was it?* He went over his inventory. *The remnant stood before him. He stood within the great dragon. His army was close upon his heels. Bob was securely within his....*

Where was Bob? He had lost track of Bob.

"Bob!" he shouted out within the vastness of the dragon.

"Yes, Master," Bob said from somewhere.

Lucifer wasn't sure from where exactly.

Lucifer reached out into the unknown reaches and felt Bob. He grabbed him, drew him close, and squeezed until Bob screeched in pain.

"You are *mine*! Never forget that! Do not wander from me again!"

Bob nodded vigorously.

"Where were you?"

Bob remained silent.

Lucifer let loose a line of expletives. "I will not be ignored, imp!" He throttled Bob's damned soul until it cracked under the pressure. "You are mine for eternity!"

"Yes!" sobbed Bob. "I am yours!"

"There is no hope for your salvation!"

"True!" Bob cried. "True!"

Normally, Lucifer would have enjoyed the agony pouring from his slave, but he couldn't properly enjoy anything at that moment. That undefined fear ate at him. He shook Bob with unbridled violence. "I have defeated God himself!"

Bob said nothing.

This silence irked Lucifer. "I devoured God's champion, his only son Jesus!"

More silence from Bob.

"Where were you?" Lucifer twisted his slave as if wringing out a wet cloth. Bob's agony dripped from him, but still he remained silent.

"Where *were* you?" Lucifer bellowed. "I will not be ignored!" He doubled the crush of his fist.

Bob fell to his knees, screaming in pain, and gasped out, "We are not alone in the dragon! We're not alone!"

Lucifer let go of his slave's soul and allowed it to flutter to his feet where it stayed, fetal positioned and nursing its injuries. He looked up and stared into the dim vastness of the dragon's interior.

He was not alone?

He forced the fear from him. He would not be intimidated. He was the all-powerful Lucifer, master of all and servant to none.

"Who dares invade my house?" Lucifer demanded as he kicked Bob away.

Lucifer waited for the reply, but no answer came. *Coward,* he thought. "Who hides within my realm?"

"The Light of the world," a voice answered this time, a confident and strong voice.

The dimness evaporated with those words and Lucifer had to shade his eyes to look upon the one who stood before him. He saw who it was for only a moment before the light took over and everything went white.

CHAPTER 92

"And out of his mouth goeth a sharp sword." – Revelation 19:15.
*

Abe stared at the dragon. Something odd was happening, something unexpected. Its eyes glowed with a white light, so bright, so pure he shielded his eyes. It seemed foreign coming from such an abomination.

Its crimson skin began to bubble and boil, slowly at first, then more quickly. Scarlet flesh fell to the earth, so hot it melted the desert sand. Open sores appeared in the dragon's hide; rays of light shot like lasers wherever the skin ripped and festered.

At first, Abe only caught glimpses of the battle that was commencing within the dragon. As more holes erupted, he could see more.

Lucifer was fighting...and losing.

The great rider who wore many crowns was there. From his mouth came a tongue. Abe leaned forward, straining to see. It was not a tongue, but a blade. It lashed out repeatedly at Satan. The Devil cursed the rider with every slash he received. Every wound left by the blade glowed with the white light.

It didn't take long for the Devil to change from cursing to begging. He pleaded with the rider for mercy. There was none. The dragon was no longer anything more than oozing, melting flesh. The battle raged on, though it was hardly a battle anymore, but a one-sided thrashing.

The rider had Lucifer by the throat. Again and again, the tongue, the blade, gashed Satan, stabbing deep, penetrating him, and leaving more rays of light with every thrust.

A horrible noise filled the air. It was Lucifer, shrieking unintelligible words. Suddenly, the light flashed. The brilliance of it knocked Abe to the ground like pressure from a tsunami. When the brilliance faded, he looked up. What he saw was amazing.

*

Splinter was speechless. He couldn't fathom what he had seen.

The rider had overcome. The inconceivable had occurred.

White light burst out everywhere. Splinter leaned away, shielding his eyes. This light was too pure for the likes of him; it stung like a million wasps.

He cried out. He screamed. He needed to escape the coming wrath.

*

JoAnne saw her opportunity as Splinter writhed. She felt his hold weaken. She wiggled free, tumbling from her mount, and she fled toward the light. She was not alone. It was a stampede, all those who had received the mark running from their captors.

*

Splinter flung a line of obscenities as JoAnne wrenched free from his grasp. He tried to reach after her, but either she was very fast, or he had become very weak. He started after her, but stopped after only a few paces. Beyond the fleeing prisoners, he saw something else. His eyes had truly been opened.

Standing behind the rider on the white horse was the heavenly host. Angels, as numerous as the sands of Outer Earth wore full battle armor with swords sheathed at their sides.

With a sound like thousands of tiny bells ringing, they unsheathed their blades. Each blade glowed white with the light of heaven. Splinter screamed. The light burned. All the demons screamed, cursing the host of heaven and the one who led them.

Among the enemy, Splinter saw Michael and Gabriel, God's mighty Generals. They raised their swords in the air and together they shouted the command that made Splinter's blood freeze. "Charge the enemy—in the name of the lamb who was slain!"

Splinter turned and fled, clawing his way in terror through the stampeding free-for-all demonic retreat.

*

Abe huddled with the remnant. Together, they watched the chaos as those who bore the mark of Lucifer scrambled toward the rider who wore many crowns. Demons, shrieking like banshees, fled the opposite direction, but they stood no chance against the army of heaven who pursued them.

In the midst of the chaos, Abe found peace. He kept his eyes on the rider with many crowns, this King of Kings and Lord of Lords. Among the crowns was one of bloody thorns, proof that He was the lamb who had been slain.

The rider looked directly at Abe. Abe found his savior's eyes to have a piercing quality, but unlike Lucifer's, he could return the stare. Contentedness and peace washed over him. Nothing would ever be wrong, ever again.

CHAPTER 93

"And the devil that deceived them was cast into the lake of fire and brimstone, where the beast and the false prophet are, and shall be tormented day and night for ever and ever." – Revelation 20:10.

*

The battle ended swiftly. Abe watched as the demon prisoners were marched by him in one unending line. The rider with many crowns raised his eyes and a door appeared, yellow with a black knob. It opened and the smell of burning sulfur saturated the air. Before the door, Lucifer struggled futilely between by two massive angels. The door opened.

"Mercy, Jesus! Don't cast me into the burning lake!" Lucifer shrieked.

Jesus said nothing. He simply motioned to the angels and they threw Lucifer through the door.

The next to go through the door was Bob, the defrocked Prophet of the Ra and former First Seeker. Once the Antichrist, he was now nothing. Despite a valiant fight, it didn't take much to prod him through.

Abe was amazed. The door was suddenly infinitely large; large enough to engulf the entire horde of demon prisoners. It sucked them into the lake of burning sulfur like a vacuum sucks dust.

*

Now there was only the angels, the rider with many crowns, the remnant of Geddon, and those who had received the mark of Satan.

Those with the mark stood trembling off to the rider's left, their faces ashen with fear. One of the group, the closest to the rider spoke up. "Lord—Lord, what about us?"

The rider answered true to the scriptures Abe had so recently learned, his voice like cold thunder. "I never knew you. Away from me, you evildoers!" and they were banished, sucked through the door to Hell.

Abe stood there with the rest of the Geddonites. They stood in utter silence for time unknown.

The rider brought Abe out from the silence. "Look behind you and gaze upon the ruins of Geddon." The rider's voice thundered, not in fury but as a gentle rumbling before a summer's rain.

Abe turned. His eyes grew wide.

CHAPTER 94

"And I saw a new heaven and a new earth: for the first heaven and the first earth were passed away." – Revelation 21:1

*

The ruins of Geddon were no more. Neither was the torn sky with the dimmed sun and the blood moon. It was all gone. In its place rose a new city, bustling with inhabitants. Abe recognized them all.

"Kerry!" he called, seeing a beautiful young woman.

"Hello Abe." Her voice was no longer that of a hundred-year-old woman, but full of youth and vibrancy like her new spiritual body.

He saw others. He knew them all by name even though he didn't recall ever meeting most of them.

There was one nearby. Once upon a time, she had been known as Nancy Love. Now she had a new name. With Kerry, she welcomed him into the city. He joined their ranks and felt renewed, knowing there would be no more pain and no more tears ever again.

CHAPTER 95

"Then we which are alive and remain shall be caught up together with them in the clouds, to meet the Lord in the air: and so shall we ever be with the Lord." – I Thessalonians 4:17.

*

The Rapture. That was what had happened.

What Abe had thought to be the devastation of almost all the Geddonites including Kerry, had been the Rapture. God had fulfilled His promise, taking them away from the coming wrath of Lucifer. Abe and the remnant had been left behind and now he knew why.

He had still been struggling in his faith. When the others had been taken, he was still considering where his loyalties belonged. Thankfully, God's mercy was on him. God knew that only by taking away everything from him, would he choose to follow his Lord wholeheartedly. He had made the right choice, and now he was forgiven and truly free.

The rider came up beside him. He was no longer on his horse, but standing beside it, guiding his royal steed. Abe looked at the rider of many crowns and many names: King of Kings, Lord of Lords, Savior of the World and more. He could see the rider was both fully God and fully human, the humble Nazarene carpenter and yet so much more.

Now, more than before, he understood the price that had been paid. The rider put his hand on Abe's shoulder. His wrists were scarred. He had willingly endured crucifixion. This was also the one who had conquered that death on the cross, by rising from it.

It seemed strange to Abe now that he had ever questioned who to follow. Especially now as he realized Satan had actually been defeated ages ago, on that first Easter morning.

Jesus took Abe by the hand. Together with Kerry, Nancy, Hunter, Nora, Garrett, Carl, Matthew, Millie, Adam, Alice and all the others; they walked further into that great city, the new heaven God had prepared for his flock.

And so begins eternity.

THE END

ABOUT THE AUTHOR

Shawn D. Brink was born in Clovis, New Mexico, but has lived in eastern Nebraska since he was five. He holds an undergraduate degree from Wayne State College and a graduate degree in Management from Bellevue University. His interests (besides writing) include church, playing guitar, and spending time with his wife and four children.

Hell on Earth is Shawn's third novel and the final installment in The Space Between trilogy. He has numerous stories and articles in various magazines and publication. To learn more about Shawn, please visit www.shawnbrinkauthor.wordpress.com

www.ingramcontent.com/pod-product-compliance
Lightning Source LLC
Chambersburg PA
CBHW070916180626
46817CB00003B/1080